THEY CALL ME THE MERCENARY

#9

**THE
TERROR CONTRACT**

Books by Jerry Ahern

The Survivalist Series
#1: Total War
#2: The Nightmare Begins
#3: The Quest
#4: The Doomsayer
#5: The Web
#6: The Savage Horde
#7: The Prophet

The Defender Series
#1: The Battle Begins
#2: The Killing Wedge
#3: Out of Control
#4: Decision Time
#5: Entrapment

They Call Me the Mercenary Series
#1: The Killer Genesis
#2: The Slaughter Run
#3: Fourth Reich Death Squad
#4: The Opium Hunter
#5: Canadian Killing Ground
#6: Vengeance Army
#7: Slave of the Warmonger
#8: Assassin's Express
#9: The Terror Contract
#10: Bush Warfare
#11: Death Lust!
#12: Headshot!
#13: Naked Blade, Naked Gun
#14: The Siberian Alternative
#15: The Afghanistan Penetration
#16: China Bloodhunt
#17: Buckingham Blowout

THEY CALL ME THE MERCENARY

#9

**THE
TERROR CONTRACT**

JERRY AHERN

SPEAKING VOLUMES, LLC

NAPLES, FLORIDA

2012

THEY CALL ME THE MERCENARY

THE TERROR CONTRACT #9

ISBN 978-1-61232-221-6

For my old friend George Smith and the men and women like him—anonymous sentinels living on the knife edge of America's first line defense—dark of the moon, buddy . . .

Chapter One

"Singing," Frost rasped through his clenched teeth. He shivered with the cold, waiting in the moonlit darkness of the stand of pines. He shuffled his feet in the snow, watching the torches of the skiers a half-mile above him near the lodge that served as center for the down-hill competitions. The one-eyed man looked around him, hearing only the wind in the snow-laden pine boughs; or, perhaps, Marlene Staudenbruch, the defecting terrorist. Perhaps her left-wing terrorist brothers and sisters who were out to assassinate her? Despite the cold, Frost pulled off the leather ski mitten on his right hand, the comparatively thin woolen glove under it the only protection against the cold for his hand. He edged the hand under his dark blue, quilted ski parka, finding the butt of the Metalifed Custom .357. His old friend and fighting buddy Ron Mahovsky had gotten the three-inch Smith & Wesson K-frame to him just before Frost had left Washington. The lanky martial arts expert and gunsmith swore by the guns and despite the fact that Frost's preference ran to autoloaders, he'd agreed to go with it—it was at once smaller and had more knockdown power than the Metalife Browning High Power 9mm Frost had left behind.

Frost's gloved fingers wrapped around the round-butted revolver, closing over the smooth finger-grooved Smith & Wesson combat grips, the gun coming into Frost's hand fully now, the first finger of his right hand already against the wide, smooth trigger.

Frost could hear the noise in the pines again—it wasn't the wind. The gun was cradled in his hand now, instinct telling the one-eyed man to cock the hammer as he would have on the Browning, but instead remembering Mahovsky's admonition to use the heavily customized combat gun's double action. Frost mentally shrugged. He'd put five hundred rounds through it—mixed plus P .38s and some .357s—before leaving Washington and the DA pull was phenomenally smooth. He left the hammer down.

Frost edged around in the darkness, still hearing the distant singing of the skiers in the torchlight parade. Silently, he thought that anyone out on a night this cold who didn't have to be was a fool.

"Herr Klein?"

Frost didn't move, his first finger tightening against the Metafile Custom's trigger for a fast snap.

"Herr Peter Klein?"

It was a woman's voice, throaty, young-sounding. He didn't like the cover name CIA had stuck him with. "Klein" meant small in German—"A small peter," he muttered.

"Herr Klein?"

"Right," Frost said, low over the whining wind, turning around 180 degrees, seeing the moonlight off the halo of blonde hair tousling in the wind. "You are—" He let the question hang.

She stepped closer, more into the moonlight. Frost saw the black-looking automatic pistol in her right hand before he saw the face, then his eye stopped on the face a second, drank it in. The photos the Company people had shown him hadn't done her justice, Frost decided. Despite the fact she'd killed at the least a few dozen people in the last three years, despite the fact she'd kneecapped people, blown up buildings, was a veritable death machine and topped the wanted lists of all the European police agencies, she was incredibly beautiful.

"Marlene Staudenbruch?"

"Yes—Peter Klein isn't your real name, is it?"

"Doesn't matter," Frost told her.

"You're right—it doesn't matter. You are to rescue me, to help me defect to your United States?"

"That's right," Frost told the woman—he rememberer her eyes were blue though he couldn't clearly see them.

"You are a professional agent for them—or a contract employee?"

"I'm not a case officer," Frost told her truthfully. "We're sort of exchanging favors."

"You have that revolver—it looks very pretty. Can you use it?"

"Try me," Frost smiled, his cheeks feeling stiff as he grinned—the cold was numbing, yet the girl looked unaffected.

"I may—Peter Klein. You are an assistant coach with the American downhill team here? Are you good as a skier?"

"You don't have to be the world's greatest doer to be the world's greatest teacher—vice-versa too, I guess. How about you—are you the world's greatest terrorist?"

"Perhaps—but I prefer the term freedom fighter. Terror is only a weapon I use."

"Why are you coming over?" Frost wasn't supposed to ask her that, but he decided to anyway.

"Personal reasons—I will betray what I must in order to stay alive, but my heart is still with the people's revolution."

"You're a Communitt," Frost stated flatly. "I don't like Communists."

"I don't like Americans—but here we are, aren't we?"

Frost smiled, taking a step closer to her. He could identify the gun she cradled casually in her gloved right hand now—it was a P '08 Luger, likely 9mm. "Not a very professional gun, lady," Frost told her, smiling.

"It shoots where I want it to and when—I don't ask for more," she observed.

"Let's get the hell out of here," Frost decided.

The girl's eyes flickered to her left, and Frost involuntarily looked that way—to his right. It was a noise, a sound like the sounds she'd made when coming up on him. But the one-eyed man was only expecting one defecting female terrorist that night and anyone else about in the trees was suspect. Frost craned the Metalifed Custom Special around toward the sound, snaking the pistol forward in his right hand.

"Let's get out of here," he snapped, dropping down to one knee and stepping into his skis, securing the binding on first the left ski, then the right. Frost raised to his full height, the ski poles going into his mittened left hand.

"You are too nervous—you are an amateur," the girl said, her German accent sounding thick and her tone sounding to him amused.

"Bullshit—it's called staying alive, girl," Frost snarled. "Come on!" Frost shoved the custom K-frame Smith revolver into the Bianchi pistol pocket in his trouser band, then dug in his poles up to the baskets in the wet snow, shoving off. "Come on, dammit!" he shouted.

Frost glanced behind him, seeing the girl pick up her ski poles. He could hear noise behind him—the metallic sound of a bolt opening, but not closing—a submachinegun. Frost dug in his poles, doing something halfway between a stem and a christie with his skis, snatching the Metalifed Custom from the holster and shouting to the girl, "Hit the snow!" He doubled actioned two rounds, fast, into the trees, then dove for the snow himself, the snow around him starting to spit up toward him, the chattering of a submachinegun bolt working coming up to him like tiny thunder-

11

claps across the snow over the singing of the torchlight skiers, but no noise of gunfire. "Silencer," the one-eyed man muttered to himself.

He fired two more of the 158-grain Semi-Jacketed Soft Points into the trees, pulling the leather ski-mitten from his left hand with his teeth, already starting to fumble with his gloved left hand for the Safariland Speed-loaders in his jacket pocket.

Frost fired two more rounds, worked the cylinder release catch, his left thumb giving the ejector rod a full stroke, then inverted the gun as he rammed the Speed-loader against the ejector star.

The girl was still on her skies, coming toward him. Frost shouted at her again as she shot past him. "Damn girl!" The one-eyed man pushed himself up on his skis, the snow chewing up under the impact of the subgun slugs all around him, isolated shots thudding heavily into the trees far beyond him. Frost pumped two more rounds from the revolver, then awkwardly got himself pointed in the right direction and dug in, glancing behind him once. There were three men coming out of the trees, each of them with the overlong muzzles of silenced submachineguns slung under their right arms.

Frost hoped they weren't good enough skiers to use the guns and cross the snow at the same time.

The girl was a hundred yards ahead of him by the time Frost got up to speed and he could see her shifting the pole out of her right hand and tucking it under her left arm, the Luger in her right hand now as she twisted around momentarily on her skis and fired. Frost dodged left, hearing the crack of the supersonic bullet as it passed him in the cold air.

Frost, his fists locked on his poles, dug in again, bending into his skis, expecting the answering shots before they came. He pulled right, then left, zigzagging as the snow chewed up around him, the bolts of the submachineguns ringing loud in the clearness of the night air. He glanced back over his right shoulder. All three of the men had ditched their poles and were using the submachineguns like balancing beams as they glided low over the moon-sparkling snow.

Frost looked ahead, almost even with the girl now. His stomach churned. A sign in Italian, German and English read, "Downhill Run—Danger—Restricted Area."

Frost's mind raced. Earlier that day, while pretending to be an assistant coach for the American team, Frost had watched Klaus Ferlach, the Austrian-born American downhill hopeful. Ferlach had taken the slopes at speeds in excess of 49 mph, beating out the East German Gaas. The run had slickened since then with the evening cold and the resurfacing work—it would be like three miles of ice and Frost realized it demanded better skiing than he was capable of.

He started shouting to the girl. There was another series of bursts from the subgunners on the snow behind him and if she heard him she ignored what he said—"Stop!"

The girl did a jump and shot up over a hard-packed drift and into the downhill run. Frost christied, pulled out the Metalife Custom Special and fired two shots, then two more, emptying the revolver's six-round cylinder and cutting down the nearest of the subgunners. The man's arms flew out from his chest, the submachinegun sailing into the air behind him. The gun, as it crashed down, impacted against the second man behind, the third man then dropping off from the run.

Frost opened the cylinder on his revolver, punching out the empties and speedloading six fresh rounds in place. He jammed the gun away into the Bianchi holster, pulled on his mittens and started around, toward the hardened drift, up and across it, airborne. There was another burst of automatic weapons fire. The clicking of the bolts without the sounds of the actual gunshots was maddening. Frost glanced down, feeling impact on his right side—his right ski pole had been shot in half.

The one-eyed man skidded down along the embankment onto the ice-crusted downhill run, sliding across his back, his elbows pushing into the glassy smoothness, frictioning against it.

Frost rolled onto his stomach. One of the submachinegunners was coming over the embankment. No time for the gun, Frost hurtled his shot-in-half ski pole through the air like a javelin. He missed, the subgunner twisting in mid-air to avoid the pole, coming down hard on the iced-over snow, skidding along on his stomach. Frost had his gun out now, double actioning two rounds into

14

the subgunner's face as the man slid past. The nose and right cheekbone exploded, blood streaking across the moonlit downhill run in a spiderweb effect.

Frost holstered the revolver, clumsily, carefully getting to his feet.

He started reaching down for the subgun the dead man still held clenched in his right fist. But the snow between Frost's reaching right hand and the submachinegun erupted.

Frost shot a glance behind him, then dug in his one remaining pole, getting off in a lopsided start, twisting his body to pull away from the embankment. He was into the downhill run now and there was nothing for him to do, he realized. There was a sick, churning feeling—fear—in the pit of his stomach as he bent into his skis, tucking the one remaining pole under his right arm.

The downhill run looked to Frost like a long, glass alley, white in the cold moonlight, the wind hammering at his face, his cheekbones feeling raw under its cutting edge. He looked back once, almost losing his balance. The third subgunner was a hundred yards behind him and closing, but not shooting.

Frost dug in his left pole, then switched it to his right hand, digging it in again.

There was a bend ahead and Frost tried slowing himself, hitting the slight rise hard, bouncing up, then coming down, his knees bending with it, aching from the strain. He could see the girl ahead of him once again, about a hundred and fifty yards. He tried shouting to her, feeling the air rushing against his mouth as he opened it, the cold numbing him, choking him.

Frost glanced back again, losing his balance, skidding laterally and poling out of it back onto the run. "Ohh!" he groaned. The subgunner was still coming, now only seventy-five yards back, the subgun slowly moving into position. Frost dug in his pole, pushing ahead, bending as low as he could into the skis and still keep his balance.

There was another bend—Frost remembered it from earlier in the day. A blond-haired man, probably German, had made the contact there setting up the meeting with Marlene Staudenbruch. It had been in the afternoon, around three, Frost recalled. Just after Frost had timed Klaus Ferlach on the downhill. And Frost remembered the bend for something else. There was a high ridge that you came over, that put you airborne, then hurtled you unmercifully into the steep straightaway for the last of the downhill run. It was built to provide maximum speed.

Frost hit the bend, thrown airborne over the hump of ice-slicked snow, hearing himself scream as he impacted onto the straightaway—"Oh no!"

Ferlach's speed had been 49 mph—the thought of it made Frost want to throw up. He could see Marlene Staudenbruch ahead of him, making a christie as she skidded in below the snow fence. "The snow fence . . ." Frost murmured under the wind pounding his face raw. He didn't think he could stop in time.

His balance was going and if he lost it travelling at the speed he had, the one-eyed man knew what would happen. He would slam into the iced-over embankments on either side of the run, break his legs, his neck, every bone in his body, he thought. Frost glanced behind him, the force of the slipstream around his body tearing at his face as he did. The subgunner was coming up fast, the SMG held like a balance beam again.

And there was the other danger if he slipped, Frost knew. It was clear Marlene was out for herself. And if Frost slipped into the embankment and didn't kill himself, the subgunner, obviously a better skier, would skid to a stop by the snow fence and finish him. His lips drawn back over his teeth, his teeth aching with the cold, Frost tucked down over his skis, head slightly lower than the trunk of his body. He could feel the wind now, ripping at him, see the snow fence seventy-five yard ahead.

Frost tried the ski pole—it broke under the strain. The snow fence was fifty yards ahead now. There was only one way he could think of to stop—a christie, but without poles he doubted he could get himself up enough to do it.

Thirty-five yards, the danger of crashing into the embankments gone, but the danger of smashing through the snow fence and into the hard packed ice-ridges beyond so real Frost could feel nausea in his throat and mouth. Twenty-five yards—the one-eyed man flexed his knees for balance. Fifteen yards. He started to jump up, pulling his weary legs and feet under him, twisting his body hard left, his legs going, the skis hitting the snow. "Too much angle," Frost thought.

"Skis too far apart!" He was sliding, skidding toward the snow fence and he threw his body down, spreadeagling in the snow, still skidding toward the fence, his skis smashing into it, the bindings releasing.

"Holy shi—" Forst snatched the Metalife Custom Special from under his jacket, his right arm shaking so badly he couldn't bring the three-inch slab-sided barrel on line with the subgunner. The man started a christie, came down, twisted on his skis like a dancer and was edging across the snow, the subgun coming on line.

Frost gulped air and smashed the base of his right fist into the palm of his left fist. There was no time for a steady hold and his muscles wouldn't take that. He snapped the wide smooth trigger once, then once again, the first round catching the submachinegunner square in the chest, the subgun flying from the man's hands, dropping in the snow, both hands slapping up against the chest. The second .357 Magnum hammered into the subgunner's throat. Frost could see the red stain there as the man—eyes wide in death—skied toward him. The momentum was carrying him, the rigidity of the body holding. Frost wrenched himself across the snow, the dead man sliding toward him, the skis coming toward the one-eyed man's face. Frost threw his arms up, over his head and face, felt the skis impacting across his back, his breath going out in a long rush. There was a loud cracking sound. Frost's breath came back in time for him to choke, cough, then vomit into the snow.

18

Frost rolled onto his back, the revolver still in his right fist, his back and shoulders aching, the breath coming hard. He stared. The dead man had impaled himself on the slats of the snow fence, one of the pointed wooden boards through his neck front to rear, another through his left shoulder.

To Frost's far right, Frost could see her, Marlene Staudenbruch, laughing, the Luger in her hands.

"You ski well, Herr Klein."

"Why—why didn't," Frost gasped, trying to stand, his stomach muscles aching so badly he couldn't. "Why—why didn't you shoot that—that guy?"

"You didn't need my help. A person should stand on his own. You did well—you shoot well. I like you."

Frost looked at the woman, then started to laugh, feeling the nausea from his knotted stomach muscles starting to come back.

"I'm sure glad you like me," Frost shouted across the snow. "And I'm gonna kick you right in the —" He didn't get the chance to tell her the exact spot then because his stomach muscles wrenched again and he lost the rest of his dinner.

"There—there, my friend," he heard her saying, feeling her gloved hand on his neck. He couldn't talk. "More of my former comrades will be coming. You should exercise more so a silly exertion like this would not so undo you."

Frost still couldn't talk, but he fell forward toward her, shoving the Luger out of her hand

and pinning the woman under him against the snow. She wriggled, trying to get free. He felt her knee smash up toward him, uselessly hitting him in the thigh. His breath finally back, Frost gasped, "Lady—I almost hope those terrorist buddies of yours get you and smoke you. You—you want me to back you up—well then damned well get on the team."

He rolled off her into the snow and stared up at the moon. He could tell right now he wasn't going to become fond of Marlene Staudenbruch. She was laughing again.

Chapter Two

Frost had almost felt surprise that the car had
been where it was supposed to have been and that
there hadn't been terrorists surrounding it. By the
time he'd circled the area in the icy cold snow,
verifying it was safe to approach the car, he'd felt
frozen to the bone. Then before entering the car,
he'd popped the hood, checking for explosive
devices. Then he'd checked the undercarriage for
a bomb beside the firewall, checked the tailpipe
for a detonating system for some bomb he hadn't
been able to find. Entering the car, he'd checked
the ignition and headlight wiring and fuse system
to verify nothing had been rigged to it. He'd made
Marlene Staudenbruch stand fifty yards back
when he'd started the car, then left her standing in
the cold, moving the car around in a large circle
just to be double sure. There was always the
possibility that a bomb had been rigged to the
speedometer, the explosives hidden somewhere he
hadn't searched; but coming down out of the

mountains, he was finally able to get the vehicle up over fifty miles per hour. By then he felt reasonably confident.

The car had been part of the plan, worked out days earlier at CIA Headquarters in Langley, Virginia. Finally out of the higher elevations, Frost closed his eye, settling back, letting Marlene Staudenbruch do the driving. But he couldn't sleep, the reason for his being with Marlene Staudenbruch in the first place haunting him.

After the convoluted attempt to assassinate the President of the United States which Frost and his FBI compatriot Michael J. O'Hara had foiled (largely by accident Frost realized),* there had been a lengthy period of hospitalization for both men. Once out of the hospital and pronounced well, Frost had been preparing to return to Europe, but not on a job for 'the Central Intelligence Agency. Rather to take up the search for the terrorist group responsible for the bombing of the London department store that had apparently claimed Bess's life. Frost had been certain she was dead until O'Hara, through FBI connections with the West German police, had produced the engagement ring Frost had given Bess moments before the bombing. The ring had been recovered from a chain found around the neck of a West German terrorist shot by police during a gunbattle. With the faint hope that somehow Bess had survived the bombing and was still alive, Frost had felt more determined than ever to pursue the ter-

*They Call Me the Mercenary #8, Assassin's Express

rorist connection. Hours before his scheduled flight, O'Hara had contacted him. Through a CIA connection, O'Hara had learned of the planned defection of Marlene Staudenbruch and CIA's search for a contract employee to get her out of Europe. Frost had applied for the job. The money was good, he reflected, but the money wasn't a major concern. Though CIA planned for him to get the woman out by a complex and partially redundant route without any debriefing, Frost had other ideas. He opened his eye and looked at the woman in profile as she stared through the windshield. She was beautiful, but from her file and from her actions on the ski slope, she was also not to be trusted—deadly was the word, he thought.

Frost remembered an expression an older woman whom he had known as a boy had liked to use—"pump". And that was his plan with Marlene Staudenbruch. To pump her—for all the information he could that could get him into the terrorist pipeline to find Bess Stallman, the only woman he had ever asked to marry him, the woman he had loved since first saving her life in Central Africa.* How long ago it was, he thought. He decided it would do no good to try to remember—remembering wouldn't bring Bess back nor bring him any closer to finding out her fate. He closed his eye again, wanting sleep . . .

See *The Call Me The Mercenary #1, The Killer Genesis*

"Herr Klein," the voice called.

"What?" Frost groaned, feeling sweat on his face and neck, his back stiff as he started to move in the front seat of the Fiat.

"Herr Klein—we are being followed. I'm sorry to awaken you—I thought perhaps since your job is to be my protector, it might interest you."

"What?" Frost opened his eye, still slouching in the passenger seat. He looked across the dashboard and beyond the hood of the mustard colored car. "What time is—" He didn't finish the question, instead squinted in the gray light at the luminous black face of the Rolex on his left wrist. It was just after six A.M. "Who the hell'd be following us at this time of the—" He didn't finish again, grunted, searched his pockets for the half-crumpled pack of Camels and his Zippo lighter, then flicked the striking wheel under his thumb, inhaling the tobacco smoke deep into his lungs as he sat up, twisting awkwardly in the front passenger seat and looking over the seat back.

"What is this, a damned parade?" Frost asked out loud. There were three cars, all driving close together in a line one after the other, the lead of the three cars a quarter mile back. "All three of them—following us?"

"It would appear so, Herr Klein," Marlene Staudenbruch said emotionlessly.

"Wonderful—that's just peachy—when did you discover this good news?" Frost asked her.

"About twenty minutes ago. I would have awakened you then, but you look so pretty when you're asleep," she laughed.

Frost glared at her, "Thanks, kid—you're really rackin' up the points, aren't you?"

"The points? Points? What are—"

"Back there on the downhill run, now the cracks—what? You tryin' to see just how far you can push me before I forget my job and put a bullet in you myself?"

"Are you always this pleasant?"

"I could ask you the same question," Frost countered, taking the Metalife Custom .357 from the Bianchi holster, opening the cylinder, checking the charge holes for six live rounds, then closing it. He searched his pockets, found the emptied Safariland Speed-loaders, then found the loose 158-grain soft points he carried. Carefully, he loaded six rounds into the first of the Speed-loaders, then pressed the flat noses of the bullets against the smooth top surface of the dashboard, twisting the locking knob at the rear of the loader in place, securing the six rounds. He began the ritual with the next empty Speed-loader.

"What are you going to do—shoot the three cars or wait for the occupants to get out, line up and raise their hands first?"

Frost glanced over at the woman, twisting the locking knob on the loader harder than he had to, silently wishing it were her throat. "No—I'm just getting ready for whatever eventuality might arise."

"Then you haven't a plan, correct, Herr Klein?"

"Correct, Fraulein Staudenbruch."

"Marlene—call me Marlene."

"I'd say the same thing, but it'd be kind of dumb for a guy to be named Marlene," Frost smiled.

"What is your real name?" she asked.

"What—you don't like Peter Klein?"

"Peter Klein—how original! You are obviously not a skiing coach—"

"You mean you could tell?" Frost laughed, looking back over his shoulder again at the three cars. They hadn't dropped back at all, but neither had they closed the gap.

"Yes—I could tell this. Who are you?"

Frost shrugged his shoulders. "The name is Hank Frost, really."

"From Peter Klein to Hank Frost—the next you'll tell me is that your name is something like George Smith. If you must make up a name, make up something original, hmm?"

"Well—take your pick. Frost, Klein, whatever."

"I like Frost better—but I still don't believe it. How did you lose your eye?"

"Well," Frost sighed, watching her as she downshifted into a curve, then upshifted again. He stared out the passenger side window. The road was still steep, a sheer drop-off beyond a gravelly shoulder strew with scrub brush.

"Well?"

"In this line of work," Frost told her.

"What do you mean?"

"Well—it's not a pretty story," Frost began.

"I can take it," the woman said.

"All right," Frost decided, clearing his throat.

"It was several years ago and fate had worked things that I was up against one of the world's top assassins—an Oriental who had been born and raised in South America. His name was Ben-Wa."

"Ben-Wa?"

"Yes," Frost said soberly. "Spent a great deal of time in Patagonia, he did—Ben Wa."

"How did this—Ben-Wa?"

"Yes."

"How did this Ben-Wa cause the loss of your eye?"

"Well—it wasn't Ben-Wa directly, rather his peculiar weapon."

"His weapon?"

"Yes—we were fighting it out and his weapon got me—knocked out my left eye. Just knocked it right out, nearly killed me."

"What kind of weapon, Frost?"

"Well, as I said, he was born and raised in South America. Spent a great deal of time with the Indians there, even worked for a time as a gaucho. He got into using the bolas."

"The bolas?"

"Three rocks, ball shaped, on long strands of leather. You hold one, twirl the other two and hurtle it. The gauchos use them like an American cowboy would use a rope or lariat. Usually, it's used to ensnare an animal by the legs. Ben-Wa used it to throttle his victims around the throat and break the neck."

"And this bolas thing—he used this on you?"

"Yes—caused the tragic loss of my eye," Frost told her, tugging at his black eyepatch, sniffing a

27

little. "Yes—and the funny thing is that to this day, I can never see a bola without thinking of that horrible instant, without thinking of the man and his weapon as one—yes. Ben-Wa Balls . . ."

"Ben-Wa Balls," she repeated, then "Ben-Wa Balls? Those are the things with mercury, that women can—You have a filthy mind!" And she laughed, this time not the condescending laughter Frost had heard from her before, or the sarcastic kind either. But simple, plain laughter. "You are insane. Ben-Wa Balls—ha!"

"Well," Frost groaned.

"Now—what are you going to do about them—those men behind us?"

"Could be women behind us," Frost remarked. "Maybe they'd be interested in the Ben-Wa Balls . . . I understand terrorist work is equal opportunity male-female, isn't it?"

"If you were as good an agent as you think you are a humorist, perhaps we would not have this—"

"Problem? No problem," Frost told the woman. "See—you have the problem. They want you, not me. All I've gotta do is get behind the wheel and roll you out the door and—"

She snapped her head toward him, her face contorted with what Frost assumed to be anger, her cheeks reddened. "You bas—"

"Tsk, tsk," Frost smiled. "No—just wanted to see how you'd like it if somebody left you in the lurch like you did me back on the ski-run—no. I'll get you through this. Or, like they say—"

A burst of gunfire from the lead car behind cut

28

him off, Frost twisting around in the seat, rolling down his side passenger window.

The girl finished his sentence. "Or die trying, Frost—hmm?"

"Shut up!" he snapped, ramming the Metalife Custom .357 out the window in his left fist, the cold air biting at him, whipping his hair around his face. He craned his neck far out, shouting to the girl, "Step on it, Marlene!" then twisting to get his right eye—the only one he had—down over his left arm. ·

He thumbcocked the revolver, aiming it for the radiator of the lead car, seeing across the red ramp insert of the front sight the black bulk of a submachinegun, maybe a Sterling, he thought. He tried bringing his fist up, getting his head down, the keep a sight picture. He fired, the revolver backing into his hand, the finger-grooved smooth combat stocks rolling in his fist. The first car—a Volvo—swerved, the submachinegun firing a long burst, the road surface on Frost's side of the Fiat taking the impact of the slugs, chunks of paving seeming to explode from it.

"Eat lead," Frost shouted into the slipstream, not bothering to thumb-cock the revolver this time, just double actioning a shot, far right, the car swerving left, doing just what the one-eyed man had wanted. Frost double actioned two shots fast, the little .357's muzzle nudging up, then up again. Frost tucked back inside.

"What the hell good did that do, Frost?" the woman shouted across the wind.

"Watch your rearview," Frost shouted back,

turning around to look himself through the rear window. The lead car—the Volvo—was already swerving toward the far edge of the road.

"What did you do?" the woman shouted.

"Only thing I could—gave up on marksmanship and aimed for the center of mass—probably punched through the radiator on one of 'em—other one probably went right on through into the engine. Can't bust a block with these .357 softies, but you can tear up some moving parts, maybe punch a hole in a battery. I could see the radiator start to spray before I pulled my head back in."

"He's still coming—looks like he's having trouble steering!"

"That's a good bet—probably power steering—if I hit the battery then it's gone, maybe hit the power steering belt. Look out!" Frost stuck his head and left hand back out through the window. The Volvo wasn't disabled, but was slowing down, making the two other cars behind it slow down as well to avoid hitting it. Frost fired again, this time aiming for the flat expanse of dark-tinted windshield. The first slug—if it hit at all and Frost wasn't certain—glanced off the winshield, doing no visible damage. Frost fired the last round in the cylinder, the windshield of the Volvo sedan spiderwebbing, cracking. The lead pursuit car was out of control now—or perhaps the bullet had penetrated and gotten the driver. Frost couldn't see to be certain. But the car was zigzagging, toward the embankment, then away from it. Then the Volvo cut away, speeding toward the rocks on

30

the mountainside of the road, impacting against them just beyond the shoulder, almost bouncing up and away from them, then streaking toward the drop. Frost pulled back inside, stroking the Metalife Custom's ejector rod, the hot nickel-plate brass empties spilling out across his thighs as he stared behind him. The Volvo hit the edge of the road, bounced up again, this time over a low ridge of rock, then down along the gravel and scrub brush. Then it rocketed into the air space beyond.

Frost jabbed one of the Safariland loaders into place, pressuring it against the .357's ejector star, the loader emptying, the six rounds falling into the charge holes. He closed the cylinder with the heel of his left hand. "One down, two to go!" Frost shouted.

Already, as Frost looked behind them, the Fiat he and the girl rode in careening near the edge of the road, he could see the second pursuit car moving up. There was a submachinegun blazing from the rear passenger window.

"Gimme that Luger!" Frost commanded the woman. Their eyes met, hers startled looking, untrusting. "Give it to me—come on!" Frost shouted again. Marlene Staudenbruch reached under the white ski jacket she wore, pulling out the 9mm.

He assumed there was a round in the chamber, studying the gun for an instant. There was still some of the "straw" coloring on it, the gun in excellent condition. He disliked Lugers though, as did most persons who periodically needed a pistol in order to stay alive. "Round already chambered?" he asked her, twisting himself over the front seat back and into the back seat.

"Of course," she sang back.

Frost only nodded to her, not knowing or caring if she'd seen him. He worked the window down on the rear driver's side. "I hope the guys behind us are real smart," he shouted, again not knowing if the woman could hear him.

The new lead pursuit car was coming up fast, the submachinegun still blazing, the car behind it closing as well, jockeying into position almost flanking the rear car. There was something poking out the rear passenger window there too—Frost thought it was another submachinegun.

"Here's hopin'!" Frost wished aloud, jabbing the Metalife Custom out the rear window of the Fiat, then firing, two-round bursts. The first two rounds visibly glanced off the hood of the lead car—a Volvo, like the car that had sailed over the edge of the road. Frost's second brace of slugs went for the windshield of the second car. He could see the glass there shattering, but the car, after it swerved hard left, came back on course. Frost emptied the last two rounds from the .357 toward the second car again, this time a clean miss. He pulled in, pulling the revolver in with him.

The lead car started accelerating—even over the noise of the wind, Frost could hear the roaring of its engine, the grinding of its transmission.

"Think I'm reloading," Frost shouted to the girl.

The Volvo was almost alongside, the subgunner starting to open up. Frost jammed the woman's Luger out the window and fired twice, then twice more, his first two rounds hitting the subgunner, the center of the man's forehead splitting wide, blood spurting out from it, streaking into the wind as the head exploded.

The second two-shot burst went through the open front passenger window.

It wasn't a clean kill, Frost thought—but it looked as though the driver had taken one, perhaps both rounds, in the side of his neck or shoulder. The Volvo veered off, toward the rocks on the oncoming traffic side of the road, the sedan climbing a massive boulder then backflipping, bursting into flames as it exploded. Frost drew his face back, heat from the explosion searing his skin.

"Two down," he shouted.

The one-eyed man speed-loaded the Metalife Custom, then slammed the cylinder closed.

The final car had dropped back, the subgunner leaning back from the window.

Frost slid across the Fiat's back seat, rolling down the opposite window, catching his feet on something near the center of the floor. He glanced down—it was the handle from a scissors jack, black and grease-smudged. "Ha, ha!" Frost snatched it up, setting it on the seat. "Here we go again!" he shouted to the girl. "Hit the gas pedal hard, kid!"

He leaned out the rear passenger side window then, snaking the Luger out, firing the pistol until it was empty, the five shots zinging audibly off the third car's fenders but doing no visible damage. The toggle action was locked open. To make sure they'd seen it, Frost shook the gun toward them, as if trying to fire it, then pulled inside, jamming the Metalife .357 out the window instantly, resuming firing. "If they fell for it once," he muttered, leaving the thought unfinished.

He pumped two rounds from the revolver, hitting the windshield of the car again, the glass shattering inward, the car swerving, but then accelerating out of the skid, still coming. He fired two more rounds, the subgunner returning fire, the rear window of the Fiat shattering beside Frost. Frost glanced toward it; he pumped off the last two rounds from the .357—again making a show of still attempting to fire the gun, then pulling back inside.

The last car was coming up fast, on the driver's side of the Fiat.

There wasn't time to reload his guns, and Frost knew they knew it, the terrorists in the last car.

The one-eyed man snatched up the jack handle, the black car with its shattered front windshield parallel to them now—almost. The subgunner was poking the muzzle of his weapon out his window, aiming to fire.

Frost leaned the front of his body out the Fiat's window, the jack handle in both his fists. He hauled it back, hearing it slam into the roof of the Fiat, then swung it forward, letting go of it. The jack handle hurtled outward, the two feet of steel slamming through the open front windshield. The driver of the car threw up his arms, loosing the steering wheel, as the jack handle impacted against him. The car shot forward, its right front fender slamming into the rear of the Fiat, throwing Frost back across the seat. He pushed himself up, speed-loading the Metalife Custom again, his knees cut on the shards of glass across the rear seat as he skidded across it.

The terrorist car was rocketing toward the near side of the road, toward the drop-off.

There was a single standing pine there, the automobile smashing into it, a body hurtling through the broken windshield, the car halting, stopping almost for an instant, then mowing over the pine tree, shooting across it and over the edge of the drop, disappearing from sight.

Frost turned around, looking at Marlene Staudenbruch in the mirror.

She laughed, saying, "That was fair, Frost—very fair if not inspired."

Frost leaned back in the rear seat. "Ouch!" He started feeling around to see if he'd impaled his rear end on a piece of glass, then eyed the woman. If he'd had Ben-Wa's secret weapon, he would have wrapped it around her throat . . .

Chapter Three

"So—you still claim you are just doing a favor for CIA, hmm?"

Frost looked across the white clothed table at the girl, smiling, sipping at the scotch in his glass. "You gotta begin almost every sentence with 'so'? What—they teach you that when you studied English in Germany?"

"I studied English in Austria—my father was an engineer and we moved around a great deal. We even lived in your United States for a time. Why do you do this favor for the CIA, Frost—or Klein or whoever you are?"

"Simple," Frost said honestly. "They're sort of doing me a favor. Helping me out on a long term project of my own." He lit a cigarette in the blue-yellow flame of his battered Zippo, leaning back, stabbing his left hand into the trouser pocket of his blue suit, looking down below the table, studying the toes of his sixty-five dollar shoes. "How come you're leaving the whatever it is?"

"The Popular Front for the Liberation of Fascist Europe."

"Ohh—catchy name. I like it—the P.F.L.F.E. Pleffey?"

"What?"

"Nothing," the one-eyed man laughed. "I've got a passion for a stupid acronyms. Why are you leaving it—what? Some sort of idiotic dispute?"

"You mean ideological," she corrected, then glared at him. "You didn't mean ideological, did you?"

"If the shoe fits, wear it, kid—hey write that down, huh?"

"You are never serious?"

Frost leaned forward, molding away some of the ashes at the tip of his cigarette. "Oh, yeah—sometimes I'm real serious, kid," he told her. "Sometimes—I'm so serious sometimes, I frighten myself with it. Why are you copping out on your people?"

"Copping out?"

"Yeah—running out, quitting the organization. You know."

"It is a personal affair—I'm, ahh—"

"Well, I don't wanna pry," Frost lied. To pry was exactly what he wanted.

"You do not pry at me—I simply feel it is no one's business why I have decided to leave my compatriots."

"Some compatriots—those clowns back there on the road to Rome weren't exactly giving you a bon voyage send-off."

"They were doing their assigned tasks in the people's revolution—I certainly cannot fault them for that."

"Nuts," Frost told her. "They were trying to kill you. They risked open assault under poor conditions on a public highway. After the first car went off the road, if they'd had any brains they would have pulled out. Then the second car? No—they want you bad and they want you fast. They could have picked a better time. They could have picked a better spot, too. Naw—they want you out of the ball game real quick. Must mean you know something really hot. What is it? I mean, just in case you don't make it and I do?"

"Then there would be less reason for you to help me to stay alive, no?" She leaned forward, Frost's eye resting on the deep cleavage of skin above the neckline of the black dress she wore. "Why don't we talk about us—where are we going, when—and do you want to come to bed with me tonight?"

"I like shy girls," Frost told her.

"I learned a long time ago that a shy girl never gets what she wants—whether it's a man or anything else."

"I guess I should feel flattered," Frost smiled, not feeling flattered at all.

"You are here—and you fought bravely this morning."

Frost glanced down at the black faced Rolex Sea-Dweller he wore—morning was a long time back. There had been the drive afterward, looking for terrorists at every turn. They had ditched the

Fiat, rented an almost identical one and driven the rest of the way to Rome from the mountains. "You plan to reward me?" Frost asked, the thought amusing to him.

"Yes—if you like? And whatever you like."

"Whatever I like?"

"Yes—whatever you like."

"Good," Frost said, smacking his lips loudly. "Well—you might think it's a little kinky," he began, whispering across the table to her conspiratorially, glancing from side to side in the hotel dining room as if to see if anyone were listening.

"What do you like?" she smiled. "Would you like me to, ahh—"

She stopped smiling.

Frost smiled broadly, feeling his cheeks creasing with it, his lips curling back. Bess had once called the look wolfish, he remembered. "Well—like I said. A lot of people would say it's kinky—but I like it."

"What is it?" Marlene Staudenbruch smiled again, sounding intrigued.

"Well—you need two pairs of shoes and—naw," and he shook his head.

"Shoes? Go on, Frost—what is it you want me to do with you?"

"Well—you'd probably say no or something."

"No—I wouldn't," she laughed. "Whatever you like—really."

"Okay—come on. I'll take you for a walk. Remember? Two pairs of shoes. I mean," he laughed, standing up from the table, setting the napkin down beside his coffee cup, then lighting a cigarette. "I mean—you can do it barefoot, but not here. Somebody might see us. Come on," he urged. "Before the house detective catches on, huh?"

Marlene Staudenbruch began to laugh, standing as Frost took her chair. "A walk—two pairs of shoes, hmm? You are crazy! And where do we walk?"

"Ohh—I guess we gotta watch out for terrorists—there's a full moon again tonight. How about we walk in the hotel gardens; that should be safe, hmm?"

"Are you a romantic, Frost? Are you?"

"One way to find out, kid," he told her. The moon would be nice, he thought, as he walked with her across the width of the dining room toward the maitre d's desk and beyond it. And the terrorists might be out as well, he supposed. But the Metalife Custom .357 was under his coat and he imagined the overly large bag Marlene Staudenbruch carried wasn't just for her hairbrush. And he wondered what was the greater danger—the terrorists or the bizarre blonde-haired girl trying to escape them. As he started along the carpeted hallway toward the hotel gardens, Frost caught a glimpse of her profile, her eyes, the bell of golden hair sweeping down to her bare shoulders. "Definitely the girl," he almost said aloud. But through the glass doors ahead that led into the garden, he saw that the moonlight had gone.

Chapter Four

"Are you afraid of a little rain, Frost?"

Frost looked at the girl, noticing a droplet of water on her nose—it looked like some sort of glistening wart and he laughed at the tiny imperfection.

"No—maybe something else."

"Me, Frost?"

There was something in her eyes, the blueness, possibly. He didn't know. The rain had come suddenly as they'd stood there in the garden, alone. He thought perhaps the other hotel guests had listened to the weather forecast. "I'm not afraid of you."

"Yourself then—that you might get to like a terrorist, a woman who shoots people in the kneecap to teach them a lesson, who kidnaps capitalist businessmen and forces them to admit their crimes, a woman who makes—"

"Shut up," he said, slowly, evenly.

"You do not—"

"Remember the woman part and forget the rest of the crap," he told her, then drew her into his arms. The shoulders of his suit were already soaking through. He wondered absently if he'd have time to dry it out before packing it in the morning.

"You are an arrogant—"

"I saw that in a movie once," he told her, his mouth inches from her face, his eye watching the water now running down her hair and streaking across her cheeks. "You know—it was this movie and the woman called the guy an arrogant something or other and slapped him."

"And what did he do—the man?"

"He slapped her back," Frost told her, bending over her, his lips touching her shoulder. Her bare skin trembled. He wondered if it was him, or just the cold rain.

"And then what did she do, Frost?" the woman asked him.

He disliked her calling him just by his last name. Bess had done that always, never using his first name that he could remember.

"She let him kiss her. I mean, she put up one of those fakey struggles, you know. Shoved her hands back against his chest, balled up her little fists and tried to push him away, but she let him anyway."

"I'll let you."

"Maybe that's the problem," he whispered, bending down again, kissing her neck. She cocked her head back, her throat bared to him and he moved his lips there, kissing her.

"Should I resist—is that your fantasy, Frost?

42

And with two pairs of shoes?''

He looked up from her neck, looked into her eyes. "No—maybe it's the fantasy I'm afraid of," he whispered. The eyes were the wrong color—Bess's eyes had been green. But the hair, the abruptness in the way she talked, the face—the one-eyed man pulled her tight against him. Her head was still cocked back, her eyes looking up at him.

"Should I resist then—should I—"

Frost shut her up the only way he could, his arms pulling her against his body, his hands kneading the wetness of her bare arms and back, the rain water mingling in the taste of her, the lips, the mouth. He felt her tongue with the tip of his own. Her hands rubbed at his neck, then he could feel them travelling down along his back.

"I should have resisted," she whispered breathlessly. "I don't want you to think I'm easy."

"You ask me if I want to go to bed—" and he kissed her neck again. "—with you. You want me not to think that you're easy. Terrific."

"Am I terrific? Am I, Frost?"

He remembered her remark from the car after he'd gotten the last of the three terrorists on the road to Rome. "Very fair—if not inspired, kid." But he kissed her again, anyway . . .

"What makes somebody become a terrorist," Frost whispered to her in the semi-darkness, the back of her neck in the crook of his left arm as they lay beside each other, Frost staring up at the

43

fuzzy grayness of the ceiling.

"To have a goal," she whispered back. "You see your goal as more important than anything else, even your life, even anybody else's life. You fight for the goal in a way that will make the world sit up and take notice of it."

"You ever hear of elections, writing editorials, public speaking?" Frost asked.

"Americans are not revolutionaries. Some Americans try to be. But you are not. Some of you feel your government is responsive enough, the rest of you don't care. I see the fascist rich destroying the world for their own gain. I see children starving in a world of plenty—"

"How are the starving children these days?" Frost asked her. "You know—I spent most of my childhood in a military school, not much time with my mother or my father. But I remember my mother once when she told me to eat some God-awful thing because there were children starving in India or someplace who would have loved to have had the food I didn't like. I told her to mail it to them so they could eat it. But I guess I really didn't see anybody starving to eat that stuff—what's bad is bad."

"But what's bad is not always bad, Frost. What's bad to one may be good to another. It is perhaps bad to murder people for political ends, but not if the ends are more important than the people blocking their realization."

"You're a Communist."

"I'm happy you noticed. But the Soviets are just as bad in their way. They have institution-

44

alized their revolution and it is no longer a revolution. The people of the Soviet Union work to perfect the revolution. The leaders of the Soviet Union simply ride along and enjoy their ease, their comparative luxury. They are as fascist as the Americans in their way."

"I'm not a fascist," Frost told her.

"All Americans are fascist," she answered.

"You believe crap like that, no wonder you're a terrorist. Americans are just like everybody else—a few super good, a few super bad, the vast majority somewhere in the middle. You look at everything as all black and all white and nothing gray—hell, that's so simplistic it stinks."

"I have seen—"

"I have seen," Frost interrupted. "I've seen terrorists like you slaughter innocent people—women, children. I've seen—" He looked down at his right hand in the darkness—he could feel it trembling when he thought of what he'd seen. The terrorist bombing of the London department store. He could feel his voice going, saying to her, "What kind of excuse is there for slaughtering civilians, people who don't have a damned thing to do with government? What kind of excuse is there for mass murder, lady? I mean, you can make one up, you can lie so good even maybe you believe it. You can turn the screws and hope to get such a wave of repression to nail you that it causes the innocent people you were killing to resist the government too. But all of that is rationalization. If I kill somebody, I don't rationalize it. If I shouldn't have done it in the first place, I don't do it."

"You have never killed somebody and thought you did wrong?"

Frost closed his eye a moment, then shook his head in the darkness. "No—but from the way you asked, I bet you did a lot."

"Shut up."

"Yeah," Frost groaned. "The truth hurts, huh?"

"You are a fool, a child. You cannot see the—"

"What? The greater goal, that the end justifies the means, that human life is something expendable for a social cause? Go line up with Hitler—that's where you belong. Maybe Stalin. Jokers like that. All you are—they were—just gangsters; you rob, you cheat, you kill, all because you think it's okay. But that's because you're nuts, wacko, crackers. You're a joke—a bad joke that makes you wanna throw up instead of laugh."

She sat up, swinging her left hand around, the hand stinging against Frost's right cheek. He caught her wrist on the back swing and threw her down on the bed, pushing his body down on top of her. "And you know something else," Frost said through his clenched tight teeth. "You're a beautiful woman, desirable—the whole shot. But if I made love to you, I'd feel like I had to wash afterwards."

Frost pushed her hands down as they clawed for his face and he got out of bed, standing by the foot of the bed, naked, then finding his clothes and fishing out his cigarettes.

He could just see her, kneeling up on the bed,

looking at him, but he couldn't see her eyes. But he could hear her voice, the voice itself sending a chill up his spine that he tried lying to himself about, that it was just the cold in the room; after all, he wasn't wearing any clothes. She was saying, over and over again, "Damn you . . . damn you . . ."

He decided not to mention to her that somebody, somewhere, years ago, had already done that.

Chapter Five

"Come on," Frost shouted into the bathroom to the girl. "The bellman got the luggage and we're set to go." His things and things the CIA people had picked for Marlene Staudenbruch had been waiting at the Rome hotel when they'd arrived. As he slipped into the tweed sportcoat, still waiting for the girl, he decided that at least that much of the action had gone right so far. His suit had been dry enough to pack. There had been more ammunition for the Metalife Custom .357 waiting with the luggage. That was also a plus.

Frost took the Bianchi pistol pocket and secured it inside his trouser band just behind his right hip, then checked the cylinder of the revolver, gave it a good luck spin and holstered the gun, securing the thumb snap. "Come on," he shouted toward the bathroom. "Venice maybe'll dry up before we get there and I'll miss gettin' a gondola ride." He let his coat tail drop over the gun, checking his pocket for the speedloaders, his wallet, his cigarettes, his lighter.

He stood in front of the mirror, pulling the black silk crocheted tie up from half mast, inspecting his new eye patch. For once he focused his stare on his other eye, and he saw a hardness there he didn't like, didn't think he'd seen before. Frost wondered—

"Are you going to make me wait now?"

Frost turned away from the mirror, seeing Marlene Staudenbruch standing by the bathroom door. "You look beautiful."

"But I'm not beautiful, of course—I'm a terrorist. That was what you meant to say."

"Yeah—something like that," the one-eyed man nodded. "Let's go."

He walked across the room, stopping as he touched the doorknob, glancing back to double check he'd left nothing behind.

"Well?"

"To Venice," he said, not smiling. Frost opened the door into the hallway. "Oh shit!" The one-eyed man slammed the door closed, knocking the girl down onto the carpet and half across the hotel room with his left hand as he swept his right hand back toward his coat, diving toward the bed. The door he'd just kicked shut splintered with submachinegun fire, the lock blowing into the room.

Frost rolled across the bed, the Metalife Custom .357 in his right hand now, the slab-sided three-inch barrel snaking forward—for the first time he noticed it. Mahovsky had engraved his name—a facsimile signature reading "Hank Frost"—on the right flat of the barrel. A smile crossed Frost's lips—it was a good thing he wasn't still telling the woman his name was Peter Klein.

Frost double actioned two rounds fast as the first of the three submachinegun armed terrorists he'd glimpsed as he'd opened the door dove through the doorway and into the room. Both shots impacted into the man's chest, the subgunner falling back, his weapon still spraying, the mattress in front of Frost bouncing under the impact of the slugs. The one-eyed man rolled left, coming up on his knees, the second man running through the door, a ski mask covering his face like the first man—now dead, splayed out in a growing pool of red blood on the carpet—had worn. Frost started to fire, hearing the sharp crack of the Luger from his left, the 9mm sound familiar to him from years of use. The second man went down.

Frost rolled again, the third subgunner firing, half stumbling across the dead man Marlene Staudenbruch had shot in the right temple. Marlene fired again, Frost double actioned two .357s from his revolver in the same instant. The subgunner's body twisted, spun wildly around, the gun firing into the floor at his feet as he stumbled forward, then fell in the puddle of blood from one of his dead comrades.

"Keep an eye on the door," Frost snapped to the girl, working the cylinder release catch on his revolver, stroking the four empties and two loaded rounds out onto the floor and jabbing a fresh six rounds into place. He snatched up the empties and the two loaded rounds in his left hand, already getting to his feet, starting for the doorway.

Frost framed himself beside it, then went through into the hallway, the Metalife Custom in both his clenched fists, snaking from side to side like a sorcerer's magic wand.

There was an old woman standing at the far end of the hall, a cleaning woman, Frost guessed. She screamed when she saw the gun. Frost let the revolver hang to his right side, muzzle toward the floor, then raised his left hand, palm outward. He moved the fingers in a little wave, saying, "I know this looks strange, but if you'd seen how big that room service bill was, you'd have overreacted too!"

He kept smiling at the old woman, not turning his head as he shouted through the doorway to Marlene, her skirt bunched up around her thighs as she came out of a combat crouch. He could see her out of the corner of his eye. "I think it's time to go, darling . . ."

Chapter Six

"I like you, Frost—I'm sorry, sorry you don't like me."

Frost took his eye off the road a moment, glancing across to the girl beside him in the front seat of the rented Fiat. "I didn't say I didn't like you. I had a teacher once—used to say something like 'I'll maybe hate the things you do, but I'd never hate you.' Sort of like that, kid," he concluded.

"Would you really feel as though you wanted to wash if you made love to me?"

There was something in her voice, something that sounded real, maybe afraid. Frost looked at her again. "Maybe I said the wrong thing last night," Frost half-whispered.

"What did you say," she asked, her voice low.

"I said—" The one-eyed man cleared his throat. "I said, well, maybe last night I said the wrong thing to you. I mean, well . . . I feel like I felt then. It's just that—"

"What?" she interrupted.

"Well—I guess maybe I'd shoot you, but maybe I don't have a right to tell you what I told you. Maybe I think terrorism stinks, but maybe—"

"What?"

"I don't know," Frost said, annoyed, lighting a cigarette as he stared ahead. "Just maybe what I said wasn't what I should have said. Maybe—Hell. I don't know!"

He was getting angry, and he didn't know if he was angry at the girl or angry at himself or angry at something else. But he knew he was angry. They had taken the back stairs out of the Rome hotel, then crossed to the front of the building where the rented Fiat was parked, and packed. No time to check for an explosive device, Frost had gambled the terrorist attackers had been confident their armed attack would be effective. With the girl beside him, Frost had taken the most expeditious route possible to get far away from the hotel, before the police would be able to piece things together sufficiently to put out the Italian equivalent of an A.P.B. on a one-eyed man and a blonde-haired woman.

The hotel bill was unpaid, but it bothered Frost little—the CIA cover who had made the reservations would get stuck with the tab for the room as well as the tab for the repairs from the gunbattle there. The room above, below and on each side of them had been rented out under fictitious names by the CIA cover as well, so Frost had no worry that stray bullets from the terrorist submachineguns had killed innocent parties in any of the adjoining rooms. What bothered him now as he drove toward Venice—aside from the mixed feelings he had toward Marlene Staudenbruch—was the undeniable fact that the terrorists knew his every move almost as soon as he made it.

At the very least, between the time he'd made the rendezvous near the ski run and the actual rendezvous itself, the terrorists had fingered him. And the terrorists had struck at the hotel at the precise moment when Frost's guard would have predictably been lowered, as he was leaving. A variety of roads had led from the Alps and Frost and the girl could have taken any of them, yet three carloads of terrorists had known exactly which road they would be on.

And the redundancy of the route itself annoyed Frost—aside from all the dead time driving. They had started in northern Italy, driven half the length of the country to Rome, then after less than a day's rest begun driving across Italy and north again, now approaching Venice. If the Company had planned it, Frost thought, to confuse any pursuers, he felt qualified to be a pursuer—he was confused.

As if she had been reading his thoughts, the girl asked, "Will you tell me now, at least—where are we going?"

He wondered if he should, then, "Well—we're headed toward Venice—you know that."

She pressed him. "What after that, though, Frost?"

He glanced across at her. "All right—as far as I understand it, we're catching a train there, the

54

Orient Express, taking it from Venice to Istanbul. Once we're in Istanbul, it's a little fuzzier. There'll be a contact, then transportation out to sea where we're supposed to get aboard a U.S. naval vessel. Where that's taking us I'm not quite certain, but eventually to the United States. Satisfy you?"

"I suppose—I have little choice."

"Then let me ask you a question," Frost began, lighting a cigarette in the flickering flame of his Zippo. "Why do you suppose the terrorists chasing you have always been right behind us? I mean, once I could have seen, but not three times so far."

He looked at her again, seeing the beginnings of a curious, Giaconda-like smile etching its way across her lips as he turned back to look at the road. Then suddenly he knew why the terrorists were so eager to risk what they had, why killing her and now killing him was of such supreme importance to them. He snapped the old cigarette butt into the ashtray, stubbing it out, then lighting a fresh Camel with his lighter. "Why did they need to have an outside-of-the-agency contract employee?" Frost asked aloud.

"You are more clever than I thought," the woman told him.

"That's why you were so interested in whether or not I was an actual agent with CIA—if I had been, you would have tried killing me yourself, wouldn't you?"

"So . . . take it a step fur—"

Frost glared at her, cutting her off. "A step further? What? Some kind of logician's exercise?"

Then Frost started to laugh, remembering the storm over phony traitors that had been used as a cover for assassination weeks earlier, and the thought amazed him because this time there really had to be a traitor—in CIA. "If I'd been CIA, you would have figured I might have been sent to get you, right? But—" He stopped again, thinking. "Back on the downhill run—that's why you didn't help me. You wanted to see if they'd actually try to kill me, to see if I was just putting up a front and worked with the terrorists. That was your set-up all the way. The ski run, on the highway, maybe even the hotel room in Rome."

"The ski run—yes. I am an excellent skier, without risking sounding conceited. I allowed myself to be picked up by their agents, to be followed to the rendezvous. If they were going to try to kill me, I wanted it there. And there too I could discover if you were—What is the Americanism for it? Sitting on it?"

"Setting you up," Frost said absently. "But we didn't get away clean enough and so they picked us up on the highway, either that or somebody in CIA found out what the Company people had planned for us and briefed the terrorists on where to find us. Same thing in the hotel room, right?"

"Probably," she almost whispered.

"So your terrorist group has someone in the Company—doesn't matter where. All he needs is the right security clearance and some nerve."

"Exactly."

"And you know who it is—and that's what makes it important enough for CIA to smuggle you out of your country against the wishes of all the European police agencies, to promise you asylum, to—"

"Terrorism—as you call it—will come to America soon, more than it has already. If CIA cannot feel that its most intimate counter-terrorist gambits are secure, it will be hopeless for them, impossible for them to fight the terrorist movement. They are fools—because it will be impossible for them in any event. I will have done nothing more than delay the sweep across America. I will not stop it by revealing the identity of our informant. My own comrades are fools for thinking my contribution of information will be anything more serious than that."

"So," and Frost mentally kicked himself for picking up the catch word from her. "So, you just got tired of running, didn't you? Tired of the wanted posters, right? You can only dye your hair so many colors, or try so many different shaded contact lenses, but after a while, all your faces would have become known, you would have—"

"Spent my life hiding in some basement, or living on some damned farm? Yes—"

"So you wanted out and used the knowledge you had of the CIA double as your ticket."

"Your CIA people had known for quite some time there was a leak to the terrorist network. They had tried using false information, all the standard ploys, but without so much as a little success. Out of desperation, when I approached them, they accepted my offer, my terms, the money I wanted—all of it. I was quite pleased."

"You wanted a vacation," Frost said aloud but to himself."

"Yes—and I'm getting it, at your expense. Clever of me, wasn't it," she smiled.

Frost looked away from her, back to the road. "Who is the guy?"

"When I lived for a time as a little girl in America, I remember an expression—that is for me to know and you to discover."

Me to know and you to find out," Frost corrected. "What happens if you get killed by your people?"

"Your American CIA is out of luck. All these nice men and women fighting to make the world safe for democracy will be out of luck."

"Shut up," Frost told her.

"Why should I? You are a patriotic American—now, more than ever, you will guard me with your life. I have no vested interest in your knowing the name of your traitor. I am revealing it only for my own ends."

"And the ends justify the means, don't they?"

"I will make a Communist of you yet, Frost."

"Bullshit," he said quietly.

"How long until we reach Venice and that train?"

"I don't know—maybe a couple of hours, then we board the train tonight. I can't figure you."

"Why—because it bothers me that you rejected me as a lover, yet it doesn't bother me that I am what you call a terrorist, or that I could reveal the name of a traitor?"

"Yeah," Frost answered, lighting still another

cigarette with the glowing butt of the old one.

"I mean—your feelings will be hurt, Frost."

"Go ahead—hurt 'em," he told her.

"I am a realist, an adult. You are like all Americans, a child. You believe that by wishing you can make it so, that by fighting hard against insurmountable odds you can always win. But you don't see—you cannot. Communism, peoples' revolutions—they are the future. It is—what is the expression, the Hebrew words, I think—Mene, Mene, Tekal Upharsin—"*

"The handwriting on the wall," Frost told her. "If you're the handwriting on the wall, lady, it's no divine message. It's just pure, toilet talk graffitti."

He rolled down the window of the Fiat some more—he wanted air.

* God has numbered the days of your kingdom and brought it to an end . . . You have been weighed in the balances and found wanting . . . Your kingdom has been divided . . .

Chapter Seven

Frost had to admit Marlene Staudenbruch didn't look at all bad as a brunette. Besides the wig, she wore dark-tinted contact lenses which made her eyes appear a bizarre shade of brown, and over these, window glass spectacles, round rimmed and accentuating the thinness of her face and almost making it appear too thin. He'd watched her as she'd made up—various things applied to her face had made her chin appear somehow thinner, her cheekbones somehow lower and she'd added wrinkle lines around the eyes and some darkness there as well to make it appear—she had told him—that she wore the glasses all the time.

Frost had been as artful as ever, he thought. He'd removed his eye-patch and substituted dark sunglasses. Rather than the CIA's plan of travelling with the girl as husband and wife, he'd let their reservations stand, setting himself up and taking the compartment they had been supposed to share, having the girl make separate reservations for herself. This latter had only been possible because she travelled with various passports. Worried at this, that fake passports she carried and the identities matching them might be known to the terrorist hit squads pursuing them, she had told Frost quite simply that she had prepared for this possibility. She had killed two women over the course of the last two months and stolen their passports, both of the women sufficiently obscure that neither of their names would be on anything but the most exhaustive list of unaccounted-for passports.

The name she would travel under was Janice Berg, an Englishwoman of German citizenship. Having no idea whether or not the deception would work, Frost and Marlene Staudenbruch—Janice Berg—had travelled by separate cabs to the railway station, boarding at separate times on separate cars, the plan not to openly communicate until reaching Istanbul. For Frost, this was perfect. He had no desire to communicate with the woman any more than necessary.

He sat now, staring out the compartment window, watching the Italian landscape changing to that of Yugoslavia, getting the cold feeling in the pit of his stomach that he always got when starting through a Communist country. Darkness was falling.

He shook his head, turning back to the paperback adventure novel he was reading and trying to lose himself in it. But he couldn't. The hero's girlfriend reminded him of Bess. He put the book down, reaching in the black nylon Safariland Swat bag and finding another book—this was science fiction. He tried starting it, tried putting his mind on the alien planet and the "shipwrecked" crew of the terrestrial scout ship wrecked there. He closed the book, glancing to the face of his watch—a half hour had passed and looking at the watch just reminded him more of Bess Stallman.

He'd made a drop on the Metalife Custom Special before leaving Venice, at a CIA cover front. Unarmed now because of the possibility of a weapon being discovered while passing through the Communist countries between Italy and Turkey, Frost felt doubly naked—if the girl were telling him the truth and her defection was linked to naming a terrorist infiltrator in CIA, it was possible that not only did the terrorists know where he was, but also knew he was weaponless.

He stood up, shivering at the thought. He decided then that if he were going to die, despite the added risk of infection if he got a belly wound, it was better to die on a full stomach. He pulled on his sportcoat, hitched his tie up all the way and left the compartment.

Trains were okay, he decided—but if it had been an aircraft he would have been landing in Istanbul by now. He shrugged mentally, walking along the companionway forward toward the dining cars.

He'd given up on the sunglasses as well, back to his eyepatch—if the terrorists were looking for him here, they'd find him despite any feeble disguise. As he sat at the dining car table—

alone—he caught a glimpse of his reflection in the dark glass. Dinner came and went and as he lit a cigarette, studying a glass of scotch, he realized he couldn't even remember what he'd eaten. He sighed heavily, leaning back, sipping at the scotch. Across the glass, but trying not to be too obtrusive, he watched the dark-haired, bespectacled Marlene Staudenbruch, sitting alone at a far end table in the dining car, eating some sort of fish. She hadn't looked at him once.

Frost decided the woman knew her stuff, perhaps better than he did.

The one-eyed man drained the scotch and flagged down a passing waiter signalling with his hand for another. He was tired, but suddenly his right eye widened—a man was walking down the center of the car, past him, as if not noticing him. The face was dark, thick featured, the hair greasy looking. But you could spot a man carrying a gun because you know where he would carry it, watch for the fall of a coat, the set of a shoulder, the way an elbow cocked. This man, Frost realized, was carrying a large sized gun butt forward behind his left hip. That spelled two possibilities, Frost realized. Either the man was a police officer or something similar with the Yugoslavian Government or he was a terrorist, and felt that in a Communist country—however far it was from Moscow line from time to time—he had a degree of impunity.

If a police or intelligence officer, he might have been there for some perfectly innocuous reason, Frost realized—something just coincidental. But coincidence, or at least counting on it, was something anyone in a dangerous business could little afford. And if he was a terrorist . . . Frost watched as the man passed the disguised Marlene Staudenbruch. He so obviously never gave her a second look, the man was either a homosexual, completely pre-occupied, neither of which Frost had read in his face, or had spotted her and didn't want to call attention to himself.

Frost decided it was the latter, pushing his chair back so fast as he stood that he almost knocked it aside. The waiter was coming with his drink, Frost brushing past the man, saying in English which he'd learned earlier the man understood, "Hold it for me—just remembered something."

Frost didn't wait for a reply. Walking past Marlene, seeing her eyes flicker up to him, then walking past her. Against his advice, she'd taken the Luger with her anyway. Something told him she was going to need it as he passed her table; he then walked through the double set of doors into the next car.

Frost glanced along the corridor of the passenger coach, seeing the greasy haired man disappearing through the next doorway leading into the car beyond. Frost followed, past the ranks of chairs, men and women sitting in them, some reading, some staring aimlessly out the window, some asleep.

The next car was a way back to the rolling hotel image so often held of the Orient Express—Frost smiled for a moment at the thought. For once something had lived up to his expectations.

He reached the opposite door, looking through the glass and following on, into the second compartment car—he passed his own compartment, the greasy haired man still ahead of him.

The one-eyed man smiled. It was a set-up. He was certain of it. The man would have other men waiting, terrorists most likely. But it wasn't a set-up to draw him away from the dining car—it was a set-up to kill him. It was too obvious for anything else. And they were banking on him walking into the trap—his eye open.

He reached the next door. There was a third compartment car and Frost started through toward it. It had to come soon, he decided. He was almost running out of train. He entered the third compartment car; the greasy-haired man was nowhere in sight. Frost could feel the hairs on the back of his neck prickling up—whatever the greasy haired man and his assumed friends had in mind—it would happen within the next instant, he realized.

Frost started through the companionway, expecting one of the passenger compartment doors to swing open as soon as he passed it. He passed the first door, walking slowly, waiting, every muscle in his shoulder and neck tensed, his hands balling into fists. Nothing.

He started past the second compartment, glancing out the window to see his reflection in the darkness—he'd always wondered how he looked when he was terrified. He could see himself, the skin of his face drawn tight, his cheeks hollowed slightly, his jaw thrust out and the lines around it hard. He rubbed his salt and pepper stubbled left cheek with his right as he walked past the second door, then moved beyond it. Nothing.

He was approaching the third door, thinking that if nerves could be physically frayed, his would be. Greasy hair would make his move, any instant, any step now, any—

Frost wheeled at the sound, the door creaking on its hinges, a hand with a silenced automatic pistol jabbing out toward him, Frost's right leg snapping back and around in a savage side kick, not at the hand with the gun but at the door, the door slamming hard against the gun, the gun discharging—there was no sound except the glass where Frost had watched his own image split seconds earlier shattering under the impact of the bullet. Frost dove for the gun, the gun clattering to the floor of the car. He felt something hammering at his back, at his neck, the gun in his right hand, his knees buckling as he stumbled forward.

He rolled, trying to remember if the gun in the split second he'd seen it had a slide lock in place. Onto his back, he stared up, one man already coming out of the doorway, wheeling toward him, a pistol—it looked like a Walther P-38—coming on line for him.

The gun in Frost's hand bucked hard once as he fired, the plopping of the apparently subsonic round more muted sounding as the round slammed into the throat of the man with the Walther.

Frost edged back on his rear end and left hand, trying to get to his feet. There were three of them now, one of them rubbing his left wrist as he started toward Frost. Frost fired the silenced pistol in his hand, the man buckling in two, falling forward, blocking Frost's gun as the other two charged for him. There was a gun in the hand of one of the men—the greasy haired man Frost had followed, the long, chubby shape of the silencer at its muzzle swinging down, lining up on Frost's face. Frost shoved frantically at the dead man who'd collapsed against him, pushing the body back, firing at an awkward angle, his shot impacting in the greasy haired man's left shoulder. The fourth man dove at him, Frost trying to snap the gun in his hand around, but the fourth man's body hurtling into him. Frost fell back onto the companionway floor, feeling the breath rush out of him, his right knee automatically going up, smashing for the fourth man's groin.

"Aagh!"

A smile crossed Frost's lips as he rammed the heel of his left hand forward into the nose of the fourth man, breaking the bone, stabbing the bone up through the sinus cavities and into the brain.

The man collapsed over him, dead, Frost still trying to free his right arm.

Greasy hair was holding his left shoulder with his right hand, the gun still in it, but the hand starting to move, the silenced autoloader starting to swing on line. Frost couldn't free his right hand, the dead man crushing it down under his weight. Frost's left hand felt across the dead man's body, under the folds of the blue suitcoat, finding something hard there, his left hand ripping open the coat.

67

There was a knife—Frost could feel the handle, feel the double quillon guard. Frost ripped at it, the knife not giving way. He fumbled by the guard, found a safety strap, tugged it free, then pulled again on the handle of the knife.

His eye caught a fleeting glimpse of the bowie patterned steel as Frost freed it from the coat, the tip of the blade catching on the coat lining, then tearing clear. A quick guess made it eight inches long.

He twisted the knife into the palm of his left hand, then snapped his hand forward, the handle sailing out of his hand, the blade planing forward, a heavy, thudding sound breaking the momentary silence. Frost's eye followed the blade, saw as the steel drove home, greasy hair stopping in mid-stride, the silenced automatic on line, the whole body going rigid.

Frost pushed the dead man fully away, clambering to his feet. He wrenched the silenced automatic from greasy hair's right hand, the man falling back, almost twirling on his feet, the face slapping hard into the glass of the nearest window, then squishing across it, blood streaking on the glass as blood poured from the twisted apart lips, the head stopping as the neck impaled on a large, jagged shard of glass still imbedded in the frame of the next window, the one smashed outward by the first bullet.

Frost half stepped, half stumbled back, the pistol in his hand—it was a Walther P-38, but marked as a P-1, apparently snatched from a West German military or police officer at one time. He

68

stared at the gun, then the four dead men.

He coughed, then lit a cigarette, the blue-yellow flame of the Zippo lighter dancing in the cold rush of air coming through the broken car window. The cigarette hanging in the left corner of his mouth, Frost pushed himself away from the outside compartment wall, his hands going to the shoulders and belt line of the man impaled on the window glass. Frost started to move the body, but then quickly searched the pockets. A Swiss Army knife, some money, a passport that looked so carefully made Frost was almost certain it was remanufactured. There was a wallet with an International driver's license, an insurance card and two credit cards, both in different names.

He debated about keeping the identification. He decided he didn't match any of the four men physically, then grabbed the first body again at the belt and collar and lifted it off the glass, pitching it out through the shot open window. He pocketed the money; then he did the same with the other three bodies, reluctantly but—he thought it was necessary—pitching the guns and knives he found through the window as well.

He stood beside the window, watching the darkness, the wind making the tip of his cigarette glow bright orange as he snapped it away, his body shaking. He looked down at his clothes—the button-down collar white shirt he wore was stained with blood from the man who'd fallen on him. Blood smeared the window as well where the glass was still in place and the unbroken window beside it. Frost shrugged—the thought had crossed his mind to clean it up, but there was blood on the carpet and the wall as well. That wouldn't wipe away. He started back through into the next compartment car forward, toward his own quarters, still shaking a little, the suddenness, the ferocity of the fight with the four now dead men having somehow gotten to him. "Getting old, Frost," he muttered to himself, stopping and leaning against his compartment door before entering. "Bess," he murmured. He smiled for a moment, thinking that perhaps—he'd go ahead and call it a miracle—that by some miracle she was still alive. And Marlene Staudenbruch was his best and only chance so far of finding out if Bess were still alive, or if she were dead who had set the bomb which had killed her.

He tried his door, the knob turning and unlocked. Frost's hands started to move into a guard position, his shoulders back, his feet squared, his knuckles burning slightly as he tensed them—"Come in, Frost—I think the deception that we did not know each other has failed."

He stepped through the doorway. Marlene Staudenbruch, the dark wig on the folded down bed, was smoking a cigarette, a drink in her left hand, her legs crossed, the tweed skirt she wore hitched half up her thighs.

"I guess it didn't," Frost murmured, walking the rest of the way through the doorway and closing the door behind him, leaning against it.

"You are very good—five men and you appear unwounded."

"Five?" and Frost edged closer to her.

"The four you killed in the next car—I saw you

getting rid of the bodies and kept watch here."

"You said five men?"

"The one in the next car ahead, with the broken neck. I pitched his body out as you did with the others."

"You killed him—the man with the broken neck?"

She looked up at him, curiously. "Of course not. I had no idea your martial arts skills were so developed. The neck was broken in one clean blow—it had to be with a bare hand. There were no other marks."

Frost sank to the edge of the bed, not looking at Marlene Staudenbruch as he pulled the tie from his neck, then tossed the jacket on the bed between them. He started unbuttoning the blood-stained white shirt, stopped to light a cigarette. "I didn't kill any fifth man, kid—we've got a guardian angel. Maybe . . ."

Chapter Eight

"How pervasive is the West German terrorist movement?"

"What do you mean?" she asked, looking at him across her first cup of coffee.

Frost was on his second, putting it down as he stared into his plate. "Remember I told you I've got an axe to grind; I'm doing this because they're—" and he avoided the word CIA. "Because they're helping me with something, a long term project of my own?"

"Yes—and now you want me to help, so?"

"Yes—so . . ."

"I do not want to help."

"Look," Frost didn't look at her, stared out the window at the sunshine on the countryside speeding past them. No mention had yet been made of five missing male passengers from the night before. He looked around the dining car then, trying to decide if his guardian angel were there, whoever had killed the fifth man. His eye stopped. A girl, very young, long hair trailing past her shoulders, dark brown and parted down the middle. The eyes looked green behind the round rimmed glasses. There was a book open on the white-clothed table in front of her, beside a pot of hot tea. But she wasn't reading the book now—she was staring back at him, the corners of her mouth raising in a smile. She nodded to him, almost imperceptibly, running the knife edge of her right hand through the gutter between the open halves of the book, then nodding again.

Frost ran his tongue across his lips, then looked away, back at Marlene Staudenbruch. "I'm ahh—" and he glanced back to the young woman with the brown hair—she was still looking at him, smiling, still moving her hand along the book in the same peculiar way she had a second earlier. He looked at Marlene again. "I—I need to know something about a particular terrorist. I mean, he's dead." Frost avoided the name.

"He's—"

"But you fail to see that if he died for our cause, then his memory will live in the hearts of the people for all—"

"Wonderful—but I need to know. Is there a connection between the West German terrorist movement and the IRA? I mean, with, say, a bombing in London?"

Marlene Staudenbruch, wearing the dark wig again and the dark contact lenses, looked at him, smiling curiously. "They are our brothers—we help them if we can."

"Your brothers," Frost said, feeling his throat

tightening, hearing his voice starting to mumble. "You said it might be possible that your brothers say, ahh—say needed you guys to plant a bomb for them, to—"

"Who is this dead man, this man you do not name?"

"His name," and Frost glanced back to see if the girl with the brown hair were still watching him. But the table was vacated, the steward clearing it. "His name was Kolner—found him dead after a shootout with the West German police."

"The pigs," and she looked as though she were about to spit.

"Whatever—what about the guy; did he work with the IRA people?"

"Never—I knew him. He never did."

"You're lying," Frost snapped, spilling his coffee into the saucer as he tried to pick it up.

"Perhaps—perhaps not. It is not your function to debrief me, Frost. I will tell what I must when I am in American hands."

"I don't think you plan to tell American Intelligence a damned thing, lady," Frost muttered, keeping his voice low so no one would hear him.

"Think what you like—it is not your job to think. You fight, to keep me safe, to bring me to where I can reveal what I know. That is all. If I knew some specific information you desired, what makes you think I would tell you at any event?"

"I don't know," Frost said softly. "Maybe—human decency?"

"You joke!" She started to laugh.

And Frost studied her eyes, still readable despite

the dark contact lenses, the window pane glasses. The laughter was genuine. "Why don't you offer me a baseball hero card, Frost—or a piece of your mother's apple dumpling?"

Frost looked at her, lighting a cigarette, his hands trembling with rage. "It's apple pie—bitch," and Frost got to his feet, the chair almost falling as he stood. He tossed the cigarette into the coffee cup, hearing the steaming sound as he started away.

Chapter Nine

"I was waiting for you to come—that is why I left the compartment door unlocked. It's Mr. Frost, isn't it? I never made love to a man with an eyepatch before."

"You haven't yet, either, kid," Frost whispered, smiling. The girl had her glasses still on, propped against a pillow in the compartment bed, a sheet drawn up over her chest, covering her breasts but the cleavage still visible. "You the martial arts whiz?"

"I thought you'd never ask—yes. Yes, I am."

"Who do you work for?" Frost asked, closing the door behind him, then locking it. He watched the muscles around her eyes tense. "Relax—if you could break that guy's neck with one blow, I'm not gonna duke it out with you."

She smiled then—a warm smile, not like the smiles he saw on the face of Marlene Staudenbruch. "I don't work—I'm a student."

"You mean there's a school that teaches riding

trains and killing terrorists and you're doing field research?"

She laughed, leaning forward from the pillows, the sheet dropping a little before she could catch it up. "No—I'm just a student, a graduate student, but not in some school for killing people. I'm taking a little trip, just to relax. I'm working on my doctoral dissertation in Field Mechanics."

"What—you learn to go out and repair tractors?"

She laughed again. Frost was beginning to like it. "No—it's, well, it's a branch of physics, very technical. I don't think—"

"I'd understand?"

"Yes," she smiled. "I mean, I'll explain it to you if you like, but I don't know how well—Are you into Einstein, at all?"

"I heard of E equals MC squared, but past that I'm lost."

"Then I don't think I can explain it to you."

"What's with the hand of death—the martial arts, you know?"

"I didn't want to get fat—I use it for exercise. I compete sometimes. I taught it for a while to help support myself—"

"You don't look like you need a lot of support," Frost smiled.

"Was that a dirty remark?"

"Your English is good—but your French?"

"Oui—but thank you. I lived in America for a while, studied there for a while. I studied English ever since I was a little girl."

"Good for you—now why'd you kill that guy?"

77

"He was following you. I started following him, sort of. He had a gun in his hand. I think he was going to shoot you. So, I ahh—I never killed anyone before. It's easy. Too easy, I think."

"Terrific," Frost told her. "Is that the truth?"

"Uh-huh."

"What's with this thing about sleeping with a man with an eyepatch?"

"I want too."

"What—you got a collection going?" Frost smiled, lighting a cigarette.

"No—not a real collection, anyway. I just decided I like you. I decided that if I sat here in bed like this and then did this," and she flicked the sheet away. The breasts were small, pretty, the pinkish-toned nipples large.

"Then what?"

"You'd want to make love to me?"

Frost shrugged, stubbing out the cigarette. "Well—you were right about that . . ."

She was beside him in the bed, but turned to face him, the glasses gone, her lips touching his cheek. "How did you lose your eye—I mean—"

"I'll tell you later."

"Did you ask the conductor what compartment I was staying in?"

"Yes."

"Do you want to know my name?"

"Sure I do."

"Veronique."

"Veronique what?"

"Guttierez."

"I thought you were French," Frost whispered

in her left ear, his lips touching it.

"My grandfather was originally from Spain—but he was raised in France."

"I knew somebody named Guttierez once," Frost mused.

"Probably not a relative—I think."

"Probably not," Frost agreed. "What do you think of one-eyed men?"

"I don't know yet."

"We'll fix that," he told her, his left arm moving around her, his right hand tracing along her abdomen, the concavity of it, the fingers of his hand stopping at her left breast.

"They're too little."

"I like them," Frost admitted, kissing her neck, his left hand on her bare behind now, stroking it.

"That feel good—when you do that."

He could feel her hands, exploring at his crotch, feel the sudden hardness he had. "That feels good—when you do that," he mimicked.

"Do you always fall into bed when someone asks you?"

"As a matter of fact," Frost murmured, his lips stopping for a moment against her cheek, "not usually. I'm old fashioned. I like to know a person a little, usually at least."

"I'm old fashioned too—it's something about you."

"Bullshit," Frost whispered. "If there's one thing I'm not, it's strikingly handsome."

"I didn't mean that—and I don't think it's the eyepatch. I just liked you."

"You pullin' my leg?"

"No—I'm pulling something else though," and Frost winced as he felt her hands.

"I didn't mean that."

"I know you didn't," she laughed.

His left hand went down to her hands, locking on her wrists.

"What's the matter?"

"Nothing," Frost told her.

"I meant what I said," she whispered, Frost taking his hand away from her wrists, feeling her hands on him again.

"What?"

"Something about you—I lie sometimes, I think most people do. But I'm not lying now. I like you, Hank Frost."

"That's good," he told her, meaning it. He rolled her over, beside him, then pulled himself on top of her. Her long hair—it reached to her waist he'd noticed earlier—framed her face against the whiteness of the pillow. The green eyes stared up at him. "That's good."

"I want you to want me, Hank—do you?"

He looked at her, then nodded his head. "Yeah—I really do."

It was partially the Staudenbruch woman, partially the feelings he had for Bess, the emptiness it had left him with. For some reason he didn't understand himself, he liked the young French girl, thought she was more than beautiful, but pretty, liked the soft, alto-like melody in her voice when she spoke. His right hand settled on her left breast, feeling the answering hardness in her, his mouth coming down on hers, tasting her, feeling

80

the warmth, the moistness. And he slipped between thighs, warm like her mouth, feeling her hands, feeling himself as he moved against her.

She screamed a little, a scream barely more than a whisper, her eyes closed, her lids fluttering as the sunshine through the compartment window streaked across the pillow, the dark brown hair and the turned up nose, the drawn thin lips. "Hank," she murmured.

Her back was arching up toward him, his left hand against it, his body pressing against her. "Hank . . ."

He felt it inside him, something exploding, felt her body tremoring under him, moving. Then he sank down on her, feeling her hands across his back, as if her fingertips were exploring each follicle of hair there. He looked into her eyes, kissed her lips lightly and whispered, "What's the box score for one-eyed men?" He realized what he'd implied, started to say, "I mean—I meant—"

"I'll swear off two-eyed men for good, Hank—and I wouldn't lie."

He smiled, kissing her again. He was the only one-eyed man on the train.

Chapter Ten

"Where were you, Frost?"

Frost looked away from the doorhandle, closing the compartment door behind him, studying Marlene Staudenbruch's face a moment. "Investigating something."

"Did you like what you found?" she smiled.

"Yes—as a matter of fact, I did."

"Why do I feel you'd rather hit me in the face than make love to me?"

"Despite your other faults, you're a heck of a great judge of character."

"I don't like you."

"At least we've got that in common," he told her honestly, crossing the compartment and sitting down on the couch-type seat opposite her.

"That young girl—is she the one who killed the fifth man?"

"Yes—claims she just did it because she thought he was going to shoot me."

"You think she tells the truth?"

"Only about some things," Frost answered. "Just some things."

Frost felt a lurch, then looked out the window.

"It's the border—the train is stopping."

"Yeah—I did the passport control thing before I came in." He looked out the window, four men standing on the smallish station platform, each of them wearing an overcoat, two of them wearing hats. None of them had luggage. "Cops—or worse," he murmured, still looking out the window.

"I'm going back to my own compartment," Marlene Staudenbruch said quietly.

"I'm going to the dining car—get a drink, maybe see what those guys are up to. Maybe Turkish cops, maybe something else."

"You genuinely hate me, don't you?" Marlene said, standing, smoothing the tight skirt she wore down along her thighs.

"No—I don't do that. I just don't like what you are. Don't have any reason to hate you personally—not yet, anyway," he added.

"How wonderfully magnanimous of you."

Frost stood up smiling. "All of us Americans are like that—wonderfully magnanimous. Comes from trading baseball cards and eating all that apple pie. You oughta try it sometime."

He opened the compartment door for her, suddenly wondering how she'd gotten into it. He looked down at the lock and saw tiny scratch marks on the lock plate surrounding the keyhole. "A hairpin," she shrugged.

"Get a haircut and you won't need 'em," he

told her, then closed the door and started to walk away, muttering over his shoulder to her, "Lock it up, huh—I mean if your hair'll stand it."

He didn't look back, walking forward toward the dining car. He wondered, crossing from one car into the next, how long he could take Marlene Staudenbruch before he did hit her, choke her or worse . . .

Veronique was sitting alone at the table he had occupied before with Marlene. Frost stopped beside it, looking down at the girl. "May I join you?"

"Have we been introduced?" she smiled.

He sat down. "Yeah—I seem to recall that we have."

"I like you, Hank Frost," she smiled. He felt her hand on his knee under the table. He reached out and touched it, saying nothing. "You look tense—I can fix that."

"I bet you can," he said. "What after Istanbul?"

"I understand there are many fine hotels there."

"Yeah—I guess there are."

"Would you like to explore one together, Hank?"

"Anybody ever tell you you're forward?"

"What is forward?"

"Fresh—you know."

"I like being fresh—do you like me that way?"

"Yes I do," Frost sighed. "Yes—I do indeed. Yes. I got things to do in Istanbul—first I mean." He looked away from her eyes a moment, feeling his smile fade. Two of the four men had entered the dining car. He saw one of them flash what looked like a badge case to an elderly man sitting at the table Veronique had occupied when Frost had first seen her at breakfast. "If I ever get to Istanbul."

"You're some kind of secret agent, aren't you?"

Frost laughed aloud, the question almost sounding genuine to him. "You're joking?"

"I mean—you're on some sort of mission, aren't you?"

"Want me to lie?"

"No—don't do that, Hank. Please."

"Then don't ask."

"We're accomplices in a murder—maybe more."

Frost looked at her, smiled. then lit a cigarette. "Try five, kid. One for you, four for me. But you were right—that guy was gonna kill me."

He watched the two assumed policemen. They would be coming to him next. "My passport and the tickets—they read Peter Klein, Veronique. Right?"

"Peter—that's a nice name. Peter . . ." It seemed to Frost that she was somehow rolling the name in her mouth, tasting it. "I like your own name better."

"Right," he exhaled hard. "Just remem—" He cut himself off, looking up as the two plain-clothesmen approached the table.

"Do you know this woman, please," one of them—dark-eyed and on the short side, asked.

Frost looked at the photo. It was Marlene Staudenbruch. "There's something familiar about the face—but I guess there are a lot of blondes. Is she missing?"

"Yes—she is missing. We wish to locate her. It is most urgent. Have you seen her, then?"

Frost studied the picture. "No," he lied. "I guess not. If I do, should I contact the conductor or what?"

"She is a terrorist, wanted in every nation in Europe. If you see her, do nothing or she will kill you. Then later contact us. Thank you," and he turned and showed the picture to Veronique. "You are travelling with this gentleman?"

Frost couldn't see her eyes for a moment—not wanting her to make a lie she couldn't support. "No—we met only a while ago. I like him very much though."

Frost smiled at that, the policeman saying, "His name?"

"He gave me the name Peter Klein," she said. The way she'd worded her answer not to lie amused Frost.

"Are you Peter Klein?" the Turkish policeman asked, turning again to face Frost.

"Would you like to see my American passport?" Frost asked, intentionally saying "American."

"No—I'm sure that is in order. It is unfortunate about your eye. An accident?"

Frost looked at the short man, then the taller man beside him. "Yes, an accident. There's an American expression about searching for a needle in a haystack. Well—it's kind of embarrassing."

"Please?"

"Well—I was making love with this farmer's daughter, see—in a haystack. Well—there really was a needle in it. Hurt like—"

"Very amusing," the Turkish policeman noted. Behind him, Frost could see Veronique's face lighting with laughter.

"Wasn't funny at the time," Frost added.

"Very well—thank you for your trouble, sir—Mr.—"

"Klein," Frost smiled. "Pete Klein."

"Yes—Peter Klein. Thank you very much."

As the two policemen walked on, Frost lit a cigarette, inhaling hard, then exhaling a long stream of grayish smoke through his nostrils.

"Is that true—about the haystack?" the girl asked him, her eyes sparkling, her face still showing the repressed laughter.

"Ohh—yeah, you bet," Frost smiled back.

He looked over his shoulder as he drained her glass of scotch. He could see the two policemen leaving the car, going forward along the length of the train.

"Thanks."

"For what?" Frost asked the girl, not thinking.

"Drinking my scotch."

"Ohh—anytime, kid." It was a matter of time, he realized, before the police, either the two men he'd seen or the other two who had been waiting on the platform with them, came to Marlene Staudenbruch's compartment. If they didn't make the identification, fine, he thought. But if something about her made them realize who she was, there would be trouble. Marlene still had her Luger in her purse or somewhere. "I think I'm going for a walk," he said absently to Veronique.

"That woman you are travelling with, whom you ate breakfast with this morning. That is the woman they are after, isn't it?"

"What makes you think that?" Frost smiled, feeling his stomach muscles knotting.

"That was a wig she wore—a good wig, maybe a man wouldn't notice it, but a woman might. A man might too, though."

"You mean those cops." Frost lit a cigarette, feeling he should be doing something, but knowing that if he went to Marlene's compartment and there were any slight suspicion of her, his being there, as if to warn her of something, would just reinforce that suspicion.

"We call them flicks, sometimes, in France," she told him.

"Flicks?"

"Cops as you call them."

"Ohh—yeah." His mind was somewhere else. He was trying to piece things together. The whole route, the needless risk of a long train ride when a midnite take-off from some back country airfield would have been better, faster, safer.

"What are you thinking?"

He saw no reason in lying. "I'm thinking I was set up, maybe you're a part of it." He watched the muscles of Veronique's eyes tensing. "I don't mind it if you're part of it—you still saved my life. I like you. Maybe you're more of a guardian angel than I thought. But something smells. With all of this, especially Marlene Staudenbruch.''

"I don't understand you."

"I think you—" The sound of the gunshot, then another and then two more cut him off. It was from one of the cars further back along the length of the train. If the train had been moving, he would never have heard it.

Frost shot to his feet, this time the chair behind him going over, crashing into a stand supporting a serving tray immediately behind him. He started past the table, past Veronique, started to fall; then, catching himself on the table edge, seeing Veronique already in motion near him.

"Whose side?" he snapped.

The girl, standing over him, her hands in a classic martial arts cats pose, her legs spread wide apart, the hem of her mid-calf length full skirt swaying over the tops of her boots, whispered, "Yours—maybe."

"What—"

"Not without me—you don't go."

There was another shot, Frost starting to his feet, the girl unmoving, her body tensed like a coiled spring. "All right, dammit," he rasped, then, his voice rising, "Come on and back me up."

He was on his feet now, and running, the French girl after him.

There was a conductor rushing toward him and Frost straight armed the man, slipping past him, the conductor starting for him. As Frost wheeled, Veronique was already lashing out with her booted right foot, a low kick across the man's thighs driving him back into the table nearest the transfer doors.

Frost half jumped over the man, passing him as he fell, Veronique visible to Frost out of the corner of his eye as he started through into the next compartment.

He stopped, staring out the glass of the windows, seeing, not believing.

Marlene Staudenbruch, the dark wig still on, the Luger in her hand was running off the gravelled embankment and into the woods, a dozen men after her. Guns were in their hands, pistols, assault rifles. There was shouting—in Turkish he guessed.

Veronique bumped into him. He looked at her, her eyes wide, the green in them seeming somehow greener, more penetrating. "I speak Turkish a little—they are saying she had killed two policemen."

"The ones—"

"No—they say something about the Englishmen."

"Shit!" Frost pushed past the girl, starting toward the car door, the girl grabbing his left arm, wheeling him around, Frost's hand reaching out for her. She backstepped, her hands in a guard position. "What the—"

"I go with you! We agreed!"

He shook his head, knowing a fight with the girl would only delay him long enough for the other two policemen aboard the train or the police outside to nab him.

"All right—dammit—come on," and Frost wheeled, starting toward the door, the short Turkish cop coming through it from the dining car, a black finished automatic pistol in his right hand. Frost slapped the gun into the compartment wall with his left hand, his right hand going forward, streaking toward the shorter man's jaw, Frost's open palm connecting, snapping the head back, knocking the Turk off balance. He could see the gun coming up, and the second Turkish policeman coming through the door. "Do your stuff, girl," Frost shouted to Veronique, sidestepping then, the middle knuckles of his right fist smashing forward into the second policeman's chest.

He started to turn, seeing Veronique going for the first policeman. The heel of her left hand streaked outward, catching the short Turk under the chin, her right hand snapping in after it, into the midsection, the Turk doubling over into the aisle.

Frost crossed the second Turkish policeman's mouth with a short left jab, the man sprawling back against the door.

Frost grabbed the man at the coat lapels, giving him a soft knee smash into the stomach, then letting him fall forward, away from the door.

Frost wrenched open the door, the police outside pursuing Marlene Staudenbruch still as thick as flies, he thought.

"This way!" he shouted to the girl, turning, starting for the platform-side door. He threw the door open, starting to jump down. There were more policemen there. He heard someone shout, in Turkish again and he didn't understand it. Two men were rushing him and Frost, his knees still flexed from the jump to the platform, wheeled, the first man diving for him.

Frost half turned left, his right foot flashing up and out, the heel impacting against his attacker's left rib cage. He could see the girl, diving through the air from the train car, the full skirt she wore billowing out like a parachute as she impacted on the second Turkish policeman, bowling him to the ground, then rolling out of it onto her feet.

More men were coming, the girl already in action, going into a flying kick, her hands hitching up her skirt high on her thighs, her left leg straight, horizontal to the ground as she flew forward, the left foot punching into the chest of the man nearest her. She was on her feet again, wheeling, kicking, catching one man in the crotch, another in the throat, the hands flashing fast as well, knuckle blows, the heels of her hands, all impacting into jaws and faces and necks, the swarming police going down as if under some sort of scythe.

Frost wheeled, his right hand flashing forward, slamming into the throat of a swarthy man coming up on his right, his left foot kicking out, dropping another man with a snap into the crotch. He spun on his right foot, the left foot working again, hammering into the abdomen of another man. He wheeled again, ducking as a drop hammer fist crashed toward his face, his left hand snapping forward into the abdomen of the man as the punch toward Frost exposed it. Coming up, the heel of Frost's right hand rammed hard into the flesh under the man's chin. Frost wheeled 180 degrees left, his left elbow crashing back into the man's stomach. Frost wheeled half right, letting the man fall, Frost's left arm already streaking forward, the inverted middle knuckles of his fist glancing off the cheek of another man, Frost's right fist hammering forward into the center of the man's chest, over the sternum. The man fell back.

Frost wheeled again, seeing the girl executing another lightning series of kicks, three men sidestepping, backing away from her, almost tripping over themselves as she seemed to herd them into her range, her left foot catching one man in the groin, her right then nailing another man in the throat, her hands grabbing the third man, tossing him in something like a half nelson to the ground, her right foot kicking out, impacting into the man's head.

Frost shouted to her. "Come on—there's a terrific part waiting for you in the martial arts movie I'm making—come on!"

He started to run along the length of the platform, turning, seeing the girl just standing there a moment, then, as if it were a sudden impulse to follow him, she started running after him. Frost almost laughed—the girl's wide mouth was upturned in the broadest grin he'd ever seen.

He shook his head, then just kept running.

Chapter Eleven

"I wish you'd grabbed a gun or something," Frost complained.

"You seem to be the professional—I'm only, what is it they say?"

"A talented amateur," Frost smiled.

"Yes—but great emphasis on the word talented," Veronique laughed.

"I don't believe you," Frost almost laughed. "But you know something? At this point in time, I don't care either."

"What do you mean?"

"If I don't find Marlene before the cops do, I've lost it. There's information she has that I need."

"For some espionage organization?"

"What—you still on that secret agent crap?"

"Well," she asked, taking Frost's cigarette from his hand and dragging heavily on it as they walked parallel to the dirt road, "what are you then?"

"Just a one-eyed man tryin' to make a living, sugar," he laughed.

"I don't believe you."

"Good," Frost laughed.

"How long before the police pick up our trail?" she asked him.

"Soon—very soon. I think we're not number one on the priorities list just yet. I don't think we killed anybody. Just maimed a few people."

"Have you killed many men?"

Frost stopped walking—his feet hurt anyway in his sixty-five dollar shoes. "I only kill women," he said, half thinking about Marlene Staudenbruch.

He wondered if Veronique read his thoughts. She smiled, then looking down at the ground, averting her eyes, asked, "Is this Staudenbruch woman such a mad dog that she—"

"Yes," he told her. "You may as well know what I'm doing—I think you do already, anyway. I was employed on a work-for-hire basis to get her out of Europe. There's some information there in her head, some information some other people need. But she's probably Europe's most wanted terrorist. I guess her own people are looking for her too. But yeah—she's a stone killer if ever there was one, I guess. Maybe like you."

It was cool as they stood in the treeline near the road, the darkness and the occasional animal noises making it seem somehow like a walk in the country gone wrong. She stepped closer to him, laying her head against his chest. "I'm cold."

"You should have brought a sweater—take my coat," and Frost began to strip his jacket off. He shivered as he placed it over her shoulders.

"Do you always—are you—"

"What?" Frost asked her.

Her right first finger was tracing across his mustache—it tickled.

"You are strong, you are tough—I like you, but for more than that. If—if anything happens to us, just remember that I like you."

Frost's guts started to churn—it was the sort of thing that seemed more than just a casual remark from a nervous girl. It was almost as if she knew something would happen and that frightened him. "What's going to happen?"

"It's just a feeling," she stammered.

"A feeling, huh? Yeah—a feeling. Well, I'll remember you like me then. Will I be in a position to remember anything?"

"Perhaps—who can say what the future holds for us. I, ahh—"

"Why did you want to come along?"

She stepped back from him, looking down to her clothes, picking a cockleburr from her skirt. "I said I liked you."

"I like you too—but that's not it. You give me all that secret agent jive—what about you? Hmm? Who are you working with?"

She looked up at him, brushing some of the hair back from the sides of her face with her hands. "I told you my story."

"You don't like to lie at all, do you. Just bend the truth? Give an answer that I could take either way and then you can tell yourself you aren't lying?"

"I don't—I don't know if I understand you."

"Most people don't," he said, lighting another cigarette, then lighting two instead, handing her one.

She took it, inhaling deeply, exhaling the smoke through her nostrils. "Someone did. You loved someone—I could tell that when you made love to me. Is she dead?"

Frost shuffled his feet in the dirt, leaning against a tree, trying to study the toes of his sixty-five dollar shoes in the darkness. "I think so—that's what I want from Marlene Staudenbruch—to know for sure, and maybe she does."

"What was her name?"

"Bess—terrorist bombing a while back in London, at a department store. I'd just given her an engagement ring. She went off to use the john, then the bomb went off. Never found a body, but they didn't find a lot of bodies—just some mangled, unidentifiable pieces. Still a lot of people missing."

"I am sorry for you—but I think I am sorry for her, too. It would be nice to love you."

"What are you talking about?" Frost asked, not looking at her.

"I said I like you—I do, Hank."

Frost turned and looked at her, tossing down his cigarette, heeling it out, then pulling her into his arms. She looked down, dropping her cigarette, then looked up at him. Even in the darkness, he could still see her eyes. "Hank?"

"What, kid?"

"Kiss me—please."

"All right—" Frost drew her closer, his hands moving along her arms across her shoulders, settling on her face, tilting her face up to him as he bent over her, touching his lips to her mouth, feeling her arms encircling his chest.

"Hank," she murmured, Frost holding her.

"Yes?"

"I—nothing, I think. We should go."

"Is that the way you want it?" Frost felt he'd played all the cards he had, that it was time for someone else to turn up a card and it would have to be the girl. If she were setting him up for a kill, he'd risk it. There was no other choice. He could wander in the woods, looking for Marlene Staudenbruch. He could make it down into Istanbul, look for her there or attempt to contact CIA. But any or all of that wouldn't guarantee he'd get any closer to her, any closer to what she knew about the dead West German terrorist and the ring taken from Bess.

He shrugged his shoulders.

"What is it?"

"I guess I figure I don't have a hell of a lot to lose anymore," Frost smiled. "Come on kid—let's go where it is we're going, let it happen, huh?"

He started walking, hearing the girl behind him. "Hank?"

He saw headlights coming down the road. He remembered her going off twenty minutes earlier, telling him she had to urinate and was embarrassed for him to see. He turned around toward her. There was a strange looking gun in her right hand. He started toward her, hearing the gun—a popping sound lighter than any silencer, he thought, feeling something sting into the left side of his neck. He kept moving toward her, reaching out for her, reaching up to his neck. She stepped back as he came for her.

There was something sticking out of his neck—and it felt like someone had given him a penicillin shot and forgotten to remove the needle. Frost clawed at the thing, ripping it from his neck, staring at it for a moment. It was blurry. Something like a dart, a feathered end fletched to it, his own blood darkening the needle.

"A damned dart gun?"

"Sit down in the dirt, Hank—you won't feel it that badly then."

"My good friend who likes me," he smiled, taking another step toward her.

The gun was in her hand again. He guessed she'd reloaded it with another dart. "Please, Hank! Don't fight it—please!"

"Bullshit," he rasped, feeling his tongue thick, his speech slurring. He glanced down at his watch—he couldn't read the position of the hands. He looked at the girl, Veronique—she was nothing more than a bunch of wavy lines, the sharpness of the details about her gone suddenly. "Veronique?"

"I like you, Hank—honestly, I do. Don't be afraid, darling."

Frost threw himself toward her, his hands going for her throat, squeezing on it. He could see her eyes clearly then. He remembered she had said she liked him. "You like me," he murmured, then let go of her neck, saw the unfired second dart poking from the muzzle of the gun as he slipped down, his hands trailing across her breasts, his right fist locking on the hem of her skirt. He tried pushing himself up to his feet, to do something, he thought. Sleep—good idea, he thought. Not a good idea, something told him. "Okay," he murmured. "So—it's not a good idea. Okay—then I'll get up!" He started to his feet, got to his knees, let go of the hem of her skirt and started to get up again. "Funny lights," he muttered, thinking about what was happening just at the front of his eye, then he fell forward . . .

Chapter Twelve

"He tried not to kill anyone—I saw that. He assumed they were your men."

"He was aiding the terrorist Staudenbruch—he is a terrorist."

"I think he is a contract employee for the CIA."

"Doing what—helping a terrorist?"

"Yes—but for some other reason."

"Believe that and you are—"

"Hey, guys," Frost groaned. He didn't bother opening his eye. He didn't know if he could anyway. "Let a guy get some sleep, here, huh?" It was Veronique talking with some man. Frost didn't care—he was too tired.

"Hank?"

"Shh," Frost whispered. He tried to roll over, but there was something tight squeezing his chest and he couldn't. He shrugged mentally and decided he could still sleep even if he couldn't roll over.

"Hank? Wake up!" It had to be the girl, he decided—unless it was a guy with long fingernails shaking him. "Take these stupid things off him, Captain Karama—now!"

"He could escape!"

Frost was very tired of having his sleep interrupted. "He's right—I can sleep just like I am. I could escape—I don't want to because I want to sleep. Let me escape later, huh, kid?"

He tried rolling over again, then remembered the thing around his chest.

"Baah," he groaned, then opened his eye.

He saw Veronique's eyes staring down at him; he looked across his chest—a big leather strap was there. He couldn't see much beyond that but he decided he was naked and the lower part of his body was covered with a blanket. Must have been wool, he decided—it was itchy. "All right—let me sleep," Frost insisted.

"Hank—don't sleep. You can sleep later. Wake up for me?"

"What—so you can pop another dart into me? Like hell, I will—now shhh!"

"But Hank!"

"Ohh—all right! Nag—" Frost started to sit up, then opened his eye wide, his head aching him, the chest strap keeping him down. He realized too then that his wrists were strapped down to something as well. He looked down along the length of his body again—he was on some sort of steel surgical table. "What's goin' on," the one-eyed man snarled, feeling his tongue as still too thick, hearing his speech as slurred.

"Captain Karama—let him go now!"

"Very well—but I shall—"

"You shall get your head broken if you don't—she's tough," Frost started, laughing.

"You are a—"

"I know—a terrorist."

"By his own admission! There!"

"Shut up," Frost snapped, at last looking at the face belonging to the voice. The man bore a resemblance to the Turkish policeman on the train—he was short, but sturdily built. There the resemblance ended, other than the dark hair. The nose looked as though it had been broken several times. The eyes were sharp, penetrating—angry-looking now but alert, searching eyes. Frost's eye travelled down to the man's hands as he undid the strap—they were big knuckles, like a man who fought a lot. Frost decided it went with the broken nose.

"There—sit up if you like."

"Where are my clothes?" Frost asked.

"They are over there—you were searched." The Turkish policeman—or was he army, Frost wondered—pointed to the far corner of the room. On a chair there, Frost saw his things.

"Close your eyes, kid—modesty, you know," Frost rasped, starting to swing his legs over the table and toward Veronique, the blanket falling to the floor. The sudden exertion made Frost's head ache, dizziness swamping over him like a wave.

"Hank—darling."

Frost looked up at the girl's face. "Why the hell did you shoot me in the neck with that dart?

Hmm? But I remembered—you like me—Glad you didn't hate me or something—would have been really tough. Probably a bigger dart.''

"But Hank—I had no choice. I—''

"You a cop?''

"Yes—a flick, really. I'm with the Surete, the French—''

"I know what the Surete is,'' Frost told her angrily.

"Then—''

"Who's this guy?'' And Frost jerked his thumb toward Captain Karama.

"I am Omar Karama, Turkish Military Intelligence.''

"That's nice,'' Frost said, sincerely.

"Hank—''

"What—what is it?'' Frost felt slightly nauseated.

"Here—have a cigarette—it will either make you throw up or clear your head.''

"Mind reading?''

"Hank—those men we fought at the railway station—they were not—''

Frost shook his head, taking the cigarette—the nausea was starting to win, but he tried holding it down.

"The young woman is trying to tell you, Mr. Frost—''

"It's Captain Frost—at least that's what it used to be, sometimes still is,'' Frost muttered.

"Captain then,'' Karama began again. "The men you fought were not units of our police, nor of our military intelligence. They were terrorists.''

"What?" Frost shook his head again, winning over the nausea.

"But not of the persuasion of your Fraulein Staudenbruch—they were the men of Colonel Dashafik, the far right, the fascist aligned—"

"Nazi, maybe?"

It was the girl who answered. "We think there are ties—we don't know for certain. But—"

"What?" Frost shook his head again, realizing he was still sitting on the end of the table, stark naked.

"There is a problem, Hank."

"Mademoiselle Guittierez is trying to tell you, Captain Frost, that you have created in our country an incident that could have the most—"

Frost cut the man off, raising his right hand, studying the glowing tip of his Camel in the left hand. "Why don't you just spit it out so I can get dressed and find a place to crash for a few hours, Captain Karama—okay?"

Frost looked at the girl's eyes, then across to Captain Karama. He was watching Karama, listening as Veronique said, "We can trust Captain Frost, Karama—he may be the only way you will have of eliminating—"

"I do not—"

"Aww—cut it out dammit," Frost snapped, getting to his feet, falling over toward Veronique, the girl supporting him a moment until he got some steadiness back in his legs. "Nobody ever finishes a damned sentence here—now tell me." He walked unsteadily across the room, leaning against the stone wall there beside the chair as he tried pulling on his underpants.

105

"Captain Frost—Marlene Staudenbruch has been captured by members of Colonel Dashafik's group. What their plans are for her besides—or before—death, I do not know."

"Wonderful," Frost muttered, trying to get his socks on without falling over. He decided to sit down.

"The terrorist group, of which Fraulein Staudenbruch is a member, has threatened that if the Fraulein is not handed over to them within seventy-two hours, they will commit a major act of violence against the Turkish state. There has already been an incident. A writer suspected of sympathies toward the faction of Colonel Dashafik has been shot in the leg—"

"Kneecapped?" Frost pulled up the zipper on his pants, leaning against the wall while another wave of nausea passed.

"Oui," Veronique murmured.

"That must happen all the—" Then Frost shut up, sitting down again.

"You work for the CIA—correct?"

Frost looked over at Captain Karama. "Did I say I did?"

"Yes—you said you did."

"Then I guess I must," Frost nodded.

"This was some sort of insane CIA plot involving Marlene Staudenbruch?"

Frost looked at the man again. "Well—I guess everyone else knows. You may as well too. The Staudenbruch woman claimed she knew the name of a left wing terrorist double agent working in CIA, probably somewhere in one of the planning

106

divisions. CIA wanted him—badly, I guess. At least that's what she says. Anyway—they offered her asylum and a new life if she'd talk. She wanted out of the Popular Front for the Liberation of Fascist Europe. I guess she was tired of running, hiding—can't blame anybody for that, even a terrorist. They struck a deal and because they didn't know who the traitor was; the CIA people hired a contract agent to get her out of Europe. Me. Trouble is, either somebody out in Langley, Virginia is a real screw-up or this was a set-up from the start and nothing I know about her is true. So—I guess your guess is as good as mine, Karama. You holding me, or can I get out of here and look for that Staudenbruch woman? Or what—am I getting kicked out?"

"I should have you incarcerated!"

"Is that a bad thing? Gotta be better than jail, huh," Frost laughed.

Karama started toward Frost, his fists knotted into balls. Frost let him come, the girl starting to scream at Karama, Frost's left foot flashing out, the only shot he could make he decided unless he wanted to fall down. The toe of his sixty-five dollar shoes caught Karama in the solar plexus, doubling him over to the concrete floor.

Frost half fell on the man, just short of a knee drop onto his back, rolling Karama over, grabbing Karama by the front of his shirt. Frost, nausea starting to sweep over him again, rasped, "Look—I don't like Staudenbruch and those creeps she worked with any better than you do—maybe a whole lot less. I'm sick, I'm tired, I've been screwed

107

by everybody who could screw me on both sides of the Atlantic and everywhere in between. I don't know why I'm here, what I was really bringing the Staudenbruch woman out for and the only thing I want is to get some damned information out of her and then anybody can have her—even the garbage man. All right?"

Karama looked up at Frost, the muscles in Karama's neck loosening slightly. His breath apparently coming hard, he groaned, "All right—yes!"

"Good." Frost got to his feet and turned around just in time so that when he threw up he didn't make Karama even angrier . . .

Chapter Thirteen

Frost had been quartered in an empty room in the officers' barracks, and after showering, discovered his clothing and other things had been taken off the train and dropped there while he'd slept. He'd taken a pill prescribed by the medical officer and slept for nine hours with it. Sitting down on the edge of the bed, fully dressed, the pain in his neck and the nausea gone, he stared down at his hands. The whole thing with Marlene Staudenbruch was insane, he decided.

Mentally, he ticked off the possibilities.

There was no CIA double—it was some sort of story Marlene had made up to still his curiosity.

The CIA double was a triple—working for both the left and right wing terrorist people in Europe. He had simply exercised the option of who to turn Marlene Staudenbruch over to.

The whole thing was a set-up from the beginning. Marlene Staudenbruch was not a terrorist travelling out of Europe into the shelter of the

CIA—she was simply another contract employee with some mission no one had told him—Frost—about, and Frost was there as icing on the cake, to make it all look real.

But what sort of mission? Was it working? Had she wanted to be captured by the right wing terrorist people? Was she really a terrorist? Was she really Marlene Staudenbruch?

And if she wasn't the terrorist Marlene Staudenbruch, wasn't part of the terror network, then all the reasons why Frost had taken the job were out the window—there would be no leads on Bess from her, for she knew nothing to begin with.

"Dammit," he muttered, smashing his right fist into his left palm, then standing up. He was hungry, but other than that well, he decided. They had given him a tetanus booster in case the dart shot into his neck had been dirty. His arm hurt from that a little. He pulled on a windbreaker over his shirt and started from the room, seeing a Turkish Army corporal at the far end of the corridor at a desk. Frost walked toward him, not remembering much of the previous evening including where to find Captain Karama.

"Hey, Corporal? Speak English?"

The young man snapped to attention, almost shouting, "Yes, sir!"

"Terrific—relax, huh? Where's Captain Karama?"

"I'll call, sir, for an escort."

Frost shrugged, not caring really. After what he considered a reasonable wait, an officer arrived and Frost accompanied him from the barracks and across a windy parade ground to a smallish, gray building. "Perfect," he muttered as he saw that was where they were headed—gray was the perfect color for intelligence work—nothing good, nothing bad. He wondered about Marlene Staudenbruch—what was she? Or was she just gray too.

Frost waited ten minutes in an outer office, Karama finally appearing in the inner office doorway, having a hushed last word with another man; this one, unlike Karama, in military uniform. As the man started across the outer office, Karama turned to Frost, then waved for him to follow inside. Shrugging, Frost followed, picking what looked like a comfortable seat—a cracked leather chair—across from Karama's desk.

"You slept well, Captain Frost?"

"Yeah—well enough," Frost answered, nodding.

"I have decided to trust you, to bring you into my full confidence."

"Where's Veronique?"

"The Mademoiselle will be joining us shortly. Does this surprise you though?"

"What—that's she'll be joining us?" Frost laughed.

"Do you deliberately," Karama snarled, "try to infuriate me, Frost?"

"I don't try that hard," Frost told him.

"I tell you that I will take you into my confidence—when I could have you shot."

"Yeah—you could. But since I'm the only person Marlene Staudenbruch—if that's who she really is—just might marginally trust, I don't

111

think you will—have me shot, that is."

"What makes you think that she would still believe in you?"

"Because she never believed in me to begin with; she knows I like her about as much as a bad case of the—"

The door opened behind him and Frost never finished the sentence. It was Veronique, rested, her hair combed again, looking as beautiful as she had when they'd left the train. She wore a gray suit—more businesslike than anything he'd seen her in—and high heels. The glasses were gone; he'd assumed she didn't really need them. But somehow the long hair still gave her the look of a grown-up little girl rather than what she was—a French cop working a special counter-terrorist detail on loan through Interpol.

"A bad case of what?" she smiled.

"Hives," Frost smiled broadly. "A bad case of hives—yes."

"Hmm," she smiled again, sitting down on a chair similar to the one Frost occupied but a few feet away from him by the opposite corner of Karama's desk.

"She trusts you then—the Staudenbruch woman?" Karama asked.

"I think so," Frost said. Then he turned to Veronique, saying, "We're discussing why he shouldn't have me shot."

"Ohh," the girl answered.

"How do you propose to take advantage of this trust?"

"I don't, Karama. Not to take advantage of it

112

at all. I've got a job I was hired to do. CIA's gonna be mad enough at me when they learn everybody in Europe knows my mission, knows what I was supposed to do. I intend to bring the girl in and you can help me."

"Why should I?" Karama smiled, almost menacingly.

"Well—you don't want a gang war between the right and left wing terrorists. If I move her into your hands, you'll have everybody tearing up Turkey. If I take her out of the country, they won't—they'll be too busy chasing me. So—the only thing you can do is help me out. You don't have any choice, pal."

"You are a bastard," Karama said slowly.

"Actually," Frost smiled. "I'm not. My father was a regular army guy, my mother—well, she was okay too, I guess. Never saw much of them, though. How about you—you a bastard?"

Karama started out of his chair, Veronique saying, "Karama—wait. Hank. The two of you fight like little boys. You should both be ashamed of it. Little more than forty-eight hours remain until the terrorist deadline."

"Yeah—that's another thing," Frost said.

"What?"

"This whole thing, this whole deal with her getting kidnapped. She shot it out with a whole bunch of people by the train. She's tough. I don't think she would have let them put the bag on her if she didn't want to."

"The bag?" Veronique repeated.

"Kidnapped, snatched—whatever. I don't think

so. She would have killed herself first. And I don't buy her story. I don't buy any of it, really. I buy Veronique—you kid," and he turned and smiled at the girl, "as a French cop trailing Marlene Staudenbruch. And I buy you as a Turkish Intelligence officer with a hot potato tossed in your lap."

"Potato?"

"A hot problem. That I buy. But to be honest with you, I don't think I've got the real truth from anybody—including the people who hired me."

"What do you mean to say, Hank?" Veronique asked.

"Well—that's it—I don't know. I was thinking about it a lot after I woke up." Frost glanced at his watch. It was already past noon. "I was running down all the possibilities. Now, if I were a detective or something, I'd probably see the whole thing, know just what's happened, the whole nine yards. But I'm not a detective, I'm not some genius at deduction or induction or whatever. All I know is that what happened ever since I started this thing doesn't make any sense to me. I mean, I'm sure it makes sense to somebody, some genius who planned this whole thing, but it doesn't make any sense to me."

"You propose that we have all been taken in?"

Frost looked at Karama—he decided the eyes were earnest, searching. "Yeah—I propose we've all been duped, as they say, made fools of. And, since I've been into this the longest of any of us, I guess I'm the bigger fool. And the only way I can see to straighten it out is to grab whoever she is and get her out of Turkey and to that rendezvous with U.S. authorities. If that's what I'm not supposed to be able to do, the best way to sort things out is to do just that—get her there. If I'm reading this wrong and the assignment was legitimate, then fine—everybody's happy. Even Marlene Staudenbruch.''

"How do you intend to find her—my men—They have been searching the countryside for her, everywhere.''

"I'm going to fall back on an old movie cliche—I'm gonna let them find me. At least I hope so.''

"Hank?''

Frost looked at the green-eyed girl. "You wanna tell me that's dumb, dangerous, the whole thing. I know it is. You got a better idea though?''

"No; I have no idea.''

"At least you're honest—but you were always that, I remember," he smiled.

"How will you make them find you, Captain Frost?''

"Well—I've got that figured out, too. At least I think I have. Depends on how secure you are that your staff can be trusted.''

"There is no question, Captain Frost," Karama steamed.

"Then you put out the word that I was arrested—make up some story. I'll help you. Then you transport me from here to somewhere else, through what you think is their territory. You put it out that you think I'm concealing some information told to me by Marlene Staudenbruch before she escaped and was later kidnapped. Then I escape, wander around and hopefully get nabbed. Not much of a plan but the best I can come up with. You got a better one, I'd love to hear it.''

Karama started to say something, but Veronique cut him off. Frost turned, looking at her. ''The only change in the plan that there must be is that not just you escape into the arms of the terrorists—I do also.''

''No,'' Frost insisted.

''I want to arrest her. We can argue about it when we reach the stronghold where they imprison her. But I am coming. There is no other way.''

Frost looked at Karama. ''I see an interesting parallel,'' the Turkish officer said, smiling for the first time since Frost had met him. ''Marlene Staudenbruch trusts you—and that is good. I, on the other hand, trust the Mademoiselle, and not you at all.''

Frost looked at the girl, then back at Karama. ''I play ball by your rules or no ball—right?''

Veronique only smiled.

Chapter Fourteen

Frost sat in the back seat of the car, staring into the hole in the darkness the twin headlights of the Mercedes bored ahead, past the backs of the heads of two Turkish Army Intelligence corporals, thinking. It was a bad plan, but the best he had; however, it was so loose, so full of potential holes, it was more akin to suicide.

Under the best of circumstances, it was bad, but with not knowing what Marlene Staudenbruch had in mind, if she were running a plan of her own, it was worse. He glanced at Veronique, sitting beside him. She didn't see him—she was staring out the window into the country darkness. He didn't know at what.

He flexed his right arm, his hand stiff a little from the pressure of the bandage wrapped around his forearm. Under the folds of bandage was a gun borrowed from Captain Karama's extensive "armory" of special purpose weapons used by his agents, this an FIE D38C chrome derringer, in the classic, exposed hammer over/understyle in .38 Special. It was loaded with two standard 158-grain round nosed leads, not a round Frost drooled over, but the best choice for the gun and inherently accurate. Frost had tested the FIE derringer earlier in the evening before leaving in the car with Veronique. At twenty-one feet he was able to keep two shot groups in the head or neck area of a full sized silhouette with good consistency.

But the FIE derringer was an emergency gun, something that hopefully wouldn't be found by the terrorists if and when they picked him up. To effect the escape, and to be taken away from him when he let himself get captured by the terrorists—hopefully—Frost had a supposedly stolen Turkish MKE, the look-alike for the Walther PP Model, chambered in 7.65mm Browning—stateside it was called .32 ACP.

Veronique was unarmed, but considering her martial arts prowess, Frost smiled, a weapon was something she hardly needed.

The driver and the second corporal beside him were not privy to the planned escape, and this worried Frost. He had no desire to kill two Turkish soldiers. But Captain Karama had insisted they be kept in the dark, warning Frost simply not to kill them, to improvise. "Improvise," Frost muttered in the darkness.

"What?"

"I was just—"

"Silence—the two of you," one of the Turkish soldiers snapped.

Frost shrugged to the girl in the darkness, not knowing if she could see him. He'd been keeping his eye on the speedometer, trying to pace the time for the designated spot where he'd effect the escape. It was coming soon, he decided. His wrists cuffed together, Frost began moving his hands to get at the supposedly stolen MKE pistol, getting it with his left hand, then transferring it into his right. He'd loaded the pistol himself, checking too by field stripping it that the gun was in working order and Captain Karama hadn't guarded against the accidental deaths of his men by giving Frost a non-functioning gun. There was already a round chambered. Frost coughed, covering the sound as he moved the slide mounted thumb safety into the up position, the little pistol now ready to fire.

He held the pistol below the level of the front seat back, the first finger of his right hand edged along the side of the trigger guard. He sighed, hard—it was time to start. "I gotta urinate—hey guys!"

"You will do this later, when we reach Istanbul."

"It must be somethin' with the water here," Frost insisted. "I've got this kind of burning feeling and—"

"It is not water that does this," the driver laughed. "It is women, my friend!"

"I gotta, though—really bad. Look, I mean otherwise there's gonna be a mess back here on the seat. I mean, it's your car and all."

"You must wait," the man beside the driver snapped, turning around.

119

"I can't," Frost insisted. "I mean, for real guys—this is no joke. I really gotta—"

"All right!" It was the driver this time. "I will stop up ahead. One false move and you will be shot!"

"Look—all I wanna do is take a—"

"All right!" The driver seemed at the edge of his patience. Frost was happy about that. Angry men usually paid less attention to what they were doing. "Here—by the side of the road. Corporal Aramanhi will get you out of the car."

The brakes screeched, the car stopping too fast, Frost swaying forward with the motion. He had the gun ready, now Veronique was ready as well. There was no barrier separating the front and rear seat, the car evidently was not used regularly for any sort of prisoner transportation.

The dome light went on, Frost squinting against it, as Corporal Aramanhi climbed out on the passenger side from the front seat. There was a button type doorlock on the back seat passenger door, the door handle removed on the inside. Aramanhi reached in, popping up the lock button, then the door opened from the outside. "All right, get out and do what you have to do. And be quick about it."

"Right, Corporal—I'll be quick about it," Frost told him, starting out of the seat, feeling almost guilty since Aramanhi's gun was not even drawn, and even if Aramanhi got the chance to go for it, he'd never make it. The pistol—Frost imagined identical to the one he had hidden between his legs—was swathed in a full flap military holster. Frost liked the design for rough use in the field, but not for combat work or duty carry. "Different strokes," he muttered. He swung his legs out, and continued swinging them, pushing himself out off the seat, his hands sweeping up, the pistol locked in his fists, the muzzle streaking toward Aramanhi's face, stopping an inch from it. "Move and you're dead, corporal," Frost rasped, hearing the strangling sound from inside the car, knowing it was Veronique using the chain binding her cuffs together to throttle the driver.

Without looking around, Frost rasped, "Didn't kill him, did you?"

"I'm checking—no," the woman's voice came back. "But he'll have a sore throat for a few days."

"Leave him two aspirin and have him call you in the morning," Frost cracked. Then, to Aramanhi, "All right, corporal—walk around behind the car with me, open up the lady's door. Hurry it up or I blow your brains out."

"I will do nothing for a terrorist," and the corporal made to spit.

Frost jabbed the muzzle of the gun an inch further forward—it touched Aramanhi's nose. "You're a brave man, corporal—I'm not a terrorist. But I'll kill you anyway, if I have to. It's your choice. I can drop you like a stone right here and take your handcuff keys and get myself freed, then free her—or you can help, then just keep right on breathing. Like I said, your choice. What's it gonna be, Corporal? If you're dead, your terrorist-fighting days are over. Who knows—if you stay alive, maybe you'll be able to disarm me. You can always try. Well—what is it?"

Aramanhi said nothing for a moment, but he didn't spit either. "I will walk around to the other side of the car with you."

"Good," Frost said with sincerity. He'd had no intention of killing the corporal at any event, and no desire to fight the man while his hands were still chained together.

Aramanhi had already started walking, talking as he moved a few steps ahead of Frost. "Where did you get that gun?"

"Stole it before we left the base," Frost lied. "Too many people there for me to try to use it, though. Figured I'd wait."

"You will never escape. You may kill me, but the Turkish army will find you and wreak a terrible vengeance."

"Scares hell out of me—let me tell you," Frost noted.

"Laugh if you will—"

"Who's laughing—now open the door." Frost stepped back as the man started to open the driver's side rear passenger door, almost knowing what was coming. It was Aramanhi's last chance. The corporal wheeled, going for the gun at his belt. Frost sidestepped, taking two steps in, using the pistol like a bludgeon and two handed, slamming it into Aramanhi's gut, the man doubling forward, Frost stroking down with the pistol across the corporal's shoulders, hammering him to the ground.

"Sorry pal," Frost rasped as he caught up the man, keeping him from falling to the ground. Frost leaned Aramanhi against the left rear fender and wheelwell, then worked the outside door handle for the girl.

"Why didn't you have me slide across and get out the other side?" She smiled at him as she stepped out.

"Why didn't I have you slide across and get out the other side, heh? Hmm," Frost pondered. "Well—I'd explain it, but you might not understand," he laughed, turning away from her and searching Corporal Aramanhi for the handcuff keys. Frost found a key ring, then on it a standard key for the Smith & Wesson Model 90s he wore.

"Here—I'll unlock you first," Frost told the girl, then twisted the key. They were double locked. He twisted the key forward first, then back, springing both locks on the left bracelet. "Now, do both of mine, then finish on yourself," he told her, handing her over the keys. The girl unlocked his cuffs with a good deal more professionalism—Frost decided that was only natural since after all she was a cop.

"Where do we go now?"

"I guess that way," Frost said, gesturing toward a rough, heavily wooded area leading up into dark, shadowy rocks beyond. "If this is—"

"Hold it," a voice shouted out of the darkness. There was a burst of subgun fire, the string of muzzle flashes bright orange in the darkness. Frost started to wheel around, the .32 ACP Turkish MKE pistol in his right fist, but there was another

123

burst of gunfire, this time into the ground by his feet "Drop your weapon," the voice commanded.

From the edge of the darkness beyond the automobile's shadowy running lights, Frost counted a half dozen men; perhaps men and women, because he couldn't see clearly enough with the light. Each of them was armed with a submachinegun. Frost dropped the pistol from his right hand, massaging his left wrist.

One of the terrorists, the face swathed with a black mask and a black scarf covering the hair, ninja-fashion, stepped toward him. As the left hand of the subgun armed terrorist grabbed at Frost's right arm, he noticed only then it was a woman. "Your arm—an injury?"

"Yes—yes, that's right," Frost told her.

She pushed up the sleeve of his windbreaker and felt at the bandage. "It is swollen. We have a doctor who may look at it. You must remain healthy for a while, Captain Frost."

"Who are you?" Frost asked. He wanted them to be the right wing terrorists, to take him to Marlene Staudenbruch.

"We represent the Popular Front for the Liberation of Fascist Europe. As long as we have you, whatever Marlene Staudenbruch has told you will not fall into the hands of Colonel Dashafik's men, and perhaps you can be used as a bargaining tool with the fascist Turkish government."

"They're not—" Frost shut up as the woman snapped the butt of the Sten gun she carried into his abdomen. Frost doubled over, more than he had to. These were the wrong terrorists, he

124

thought. "Dammit," he muttered.

"Silence," the woman commanded. The one-eyed man felt he was getting tired of people telling him to shut up that night.

"Come; we will take you to the people's prison."

Frost looked at her. "What—people's prison? Is that a chain, or are they independently franchised?"

"Silence," she commanded again, the Sten gun ramming into his abdomen again. He looked up at the woman and only smiled; he wondered just how much finger pressure it would take to snap her neck. "You and the woman will come with us!"

Frost felt her hand shove at his back, wanted to break her neck then, but realized the timing would be bad. He started walking—waiting.

He caught a flash of light in Veronique's green eyes for an instant. He decided then that as far as killing the terrorist with the submachinegun walking immediately behind him now was concerned, he might have to take a number.

Chapter Fifteen

Frost and the girl had been forced to strip naked when they'd finally reached the "people's prison," a chateau-like house in the foothills, isolated in a rocky area with a commanding view of all four sides of the valley below and the peaks above. After the disrobed search, then a search of their clothes for weapons, they had been allowed to dress again. Frost's bandage had not been touched, and the tiny FIE .38 Special derringer was still in place. Not a word had been said as the lightbulb had been removed from the single bulb ceiling fixture, plunging the room into darkness save for the single beam of an angle head flashlight. Then the terrorist holding the flashight—the same woman Frost had decided to choke to death earlier—had backed out of the room, pulling the door closed behind her, the light from the flashlight vanishing simultaneously with the sound of the bolt on the outside of the door being slammed home.

"Well—looks like it's a great success so far," Frost murmured, reaching out into the darkness and taking the girl's arm—feeling it tense for an instant, then relax as she stepped beside him. The room seemed like a closet on the dark side of the moon, Frost thought: he could see nothing, not even shadow.

"They will try to kill us soon, I think."

"Not too soon, but soon. They'll want to make us worry a lot first; but you're right. I don't think they'll wait too long, just because they want to talk with us and find out what they can about Marlene Staudenbruch."

She leaned up to him—he could feel the movement, feel her lips touching his left ear. "When are you going to use that gun?" she whispered.

"I don't know," he whispered back. "When the situation looks right—just follow my lead. Same to you—you're no amateur. If you get a chance, make your play and I'll back you up. Whatever works—I'm not that chauvinistic."

"I like you, Hank—I still do. I hope we can make love again."

"We could now," Frost whispered, his fingers feeling her breasts under the fabric of her blouse.

"They might be watching."

"I'm sure they could stand a relief of the boredom—must be damned dull around here."

"Later? Please?"

"All right," Frost told her. "Let's find a wall and sit down beside it. Remember—when they open the door, chances are they'll have a floodlight of some kind, to blind us in case we're ready

127

with some kind of play. When you hear the door, close your eyes."

"All right, I will. Hank?"

"Yeah?"

"They wouldn't just leave us here to die? Would they?"

"No, if this goes much over a couple of hours, I'll start on the door. Don't worry. They've got a time limit and they know we know it—they're just trying to shake us a little."

"They do a good job, n'es-ce pas?"

Frost laughed, murmuring, "Not bad for amateurs. You always gotta watch amateurs though. Big problem with terrorists. Amateurs with professional skills—worse than professionals like us. Meaner, too. They do what they do because they enjoy it."

"Interpol—a flash from them labelled you as a mercenary soldier sometimes."

"Mercenary? Some people say I'm that—some people say lots worse, though."

"The story about the girl—Bess? It was true?"

"Yes—come on," and Frost started moving slowly through the darkness toward what he thought was the direction of the far wall, picking his steps, holding the girl's elbow to guide her. If he'd had his lighter, he would have used it. They hadn't taken his watch, though, and the luminous face of the Rolex glowed like a beacon in the otherwise total darkness.

"I hope you find she is still alive—but I will miss you."

"I'll miss you too—but you're too young for me."

128

"How old do you think I am?" she asked.

"Twenty-six, maybe," he told her.

"I am twenty-seven. You make me younger than I am."

"I was born in 1946—figure that out," Frost whispered.

"That is not—"

"Isn't exactly young, either," he reminded her. "But you're sweet to think it."

"Hank—maybe we can just a little now," she said, stopping beside him as he halted, his hand reaching the wall.

"What?"

"Make love, Hank—maybe a little?"

"All right," he told her, pulling her closer to him. His right hand searched along her thigh, found a fold of her full skirt and pulled it up, then his hand slipped under it. "All right," and he kissed her then brought her down on the floor beside him . . .

Frost only realized they'd fallen asleep when he heard the rattling at the outside door. He opened his eye, his right arm stiff with the girl sleeping in it, her head against his shoulder. "They're coming," Frost rasped, shaking her. He could feel her coming instantly awake.

He held his right fist balled over his good eye as the light swept them, a light as bright as staring into the sun it seemed after the prolonged period of total darkness. "On your feet—up!"

Still squinting against the light, he could feel hands touching at his shoulders, jerking him roughly to his feet. He could see a little with his eye squinted tight. There were six of them, at least two of them women, all armed with submachine-guns, all with the black cloth-ski-mask like toques over their heads, covering their faces. "On your feet, pig!"

"Now," Frost snapped, almost quietly, his right knee smashing up into the groin of the person nearest him—he hoped it was a man, the little der-ringer pistol in his left fist, the hammer already at full stand. He rammed the pistol out at arm's length, the muzzle of it less than a yard from the hooded face of one of the other terrorists, the pis-tol bucking once in his hand as it fired. The top of the terrorist's head seemed to explode upward, Frost swinging the gun on line with the next nearest hooded face, his left thumb cocking the FIE derringer again. He heard a scream—one of the women, probably Veronique getting her, Frost thought, but didn't look to see.

He fired the little two shot O/U derringer again, the terrorist's black gloved right hand apparently dropping a submachinegun—the sound of it clat-tering to the floor almost drowned out in the scream as the terrorist grabbed for his neck. Frost's right foot lashed out, in a high sweeping kick, the arch of his foot smashing into the rib-cage of one of the other terrorists, then his left fist hammering forward, the pistol—empty now—like a roll of quarters in his hand as he laced the hooded face with the base of his fist, the butt of the tiny pistol hooking into something under the hood that almost had to be a nose.

By now, Frost could see Veronique, one body

down beside her feet but not near enough that were there still life in it, she'd be vulnerable to a sweep. Her left foot flashed up, outward, the hooded figure sidestepping, trying to bring the submachinegun up and into a firing position. But Veronique wheeled, turning around almost a full 360 degrees, her booted right foot kicking up and out, almost slapping at the hooded face on the backswing. As the figure she fought started tumbling back, she closed, the middle knuckles of her right hand hammering square into the center of the facial area, the left hand grasping at the throat, seeming to pull, twist and rip. The hooded figure collapsed like a bundle of rags.

Frost scanned the floor, one of the submachineguns in his hands now, the only one of the hooded terrorists still moving, the one he'd kneed in the groin when he'd first made his play.

Frost looked at the man, then rasped, "Sorry pal," then kicked the hooded figure in the right side of the head. "Hope he didn't have someplace to go," Frost smiled.

"Are you sure it was a man?" Veronique asked, breathless.

Frost looked at her. There was a submachinegun in her hands as well. "Yeah—never get a rear end like that on a woman," and Frost nodded toward the unconscious figure. "Get to the door and take another one of these," and Frost handed her another of the Sten guns. "First somebody comes, start throwin' lead. I'll be with you in a minute."

He could hear the clicking sound of the girl's

131

high heeled boots across the stone floor as he bent to the nearest of the hooded figures. Methodically, he would rip the hood away, search the body for weapons, ammunition, anything useful, then move along to the next. Three of them had been women. Two out of the six were still alive, but only one looked to make it, the one Frost had kicked in the head. The second one was paralyzed by one of the karate blows—Frost couldn't honestly remember if he had done it or Veronique—and was suffocating, already in a coma. Nothing to do for the woman, Frost propped the head along the thigh of one of the others and left her there, taking the other injured one, the man Frost had kicked, binding his hands and feet and gagging him. By the time Frost looked back to the woman who had been suffocating, she was already dead. "Five," he muttered, then shook his head. Most of them had been what he would have labelled kids—but perverted kids who thought the answer to the world's problems was to kneecap old men and blow up women and babies.

His belt stuffed with pistols, his pockets stuffed with knives and spare ammo, he walked across the stone floor to the doorway, four submachineguns cradled in his arms. "There is no one coming," the girl said, looking at him, almost puzzled, he felt.

"I don't think there was anyone to come. Look out there. See—no more than three cars. There were five cars when we came up. I think they'd decided they weren't going to question us, just kill us. That's why I made my play when I did." Frost set the subguns down, then found the little derringer in the left outside pocket of his windbreaker. "I'll have to buy myself one of these—worked out okay," he smiled, flipping the emptied little gun in his hand.

"We are alone here?"

"I think so," Frost told her.

"Why had they decided to kill us?"

"Maybe someone of them got the same idea I had before—this is the giant set-up that attacked the earth. Come on, take what strikes your fancy, help me neutralize the rest of the guns and we'll do the same with the cars, then hit the road to Istanbul."

"What is in Istanbul?"

"Lots of great stuff—the St. Sophia Mosque, the Topkapi palace, the—"

"Hank—what is in Istanbul?"

"If these guys kneecapped that right wing journalist, like Karama said they did, then he's the only lead we've got left."

"He'll be in a hospital, under guard, Hank—we can't—"

"I sure hope we can," Frost told her, smiling, then checking through the pistols as he laid them out on the floor. There was a blue worn tangent rear sight Browning High Power with a slot in the grip backstrap for a shoulder stock. He dumped the magazine, cleared the chamber and replaced the magazine to try the trigger pull—the magazine safety was still functional. The trigger didn't whish off like the worked-over Metalifed High Power he'd left back stateside, but it would do the job, he decided. There were four extra magazines and he took these, then scrounged the other three 9mm pistols—a Beretta Brigadier, a Walther P-38 and a Colt Combat Commander—for the ammo, all of it solids. "You can't have everything," he muttered to the girl.

Chapter Sixteen

"If he was important enough to shoot to drive
the point home with Dashafik's men, he may have
been important enough to know something. At
least I hope so," Frost told her. "There's one—go
get her, kid."

Veronique was out of the car the next instant,
Frost having taped over the dome light with a roll
of electrical tape from the trunk tool kit, the car
now in total darkness in the alley a block from the
closely guarded hospital. Veronique streaked
across the alley, changed in the back seat of the
car to one of the black, ninja-like outfits the terrorists had worn, now barely discernible as a
darker shadow among a myriad of shadows as she
caught the blue-caped, white-uniformed, white-
capped nurse crossing at the end of the alley. Frost
could see the black shadow that was Veronique,
seemingly smothering the nurse, dragging her into
the alley, the body going limp. Frost was out of
the car then, running down the alley.

"Help me get her into the car," Veronique ordered.

"Right," Frost muttered, snatching the woman up into his arms and carrying her, Veronique beside him.

"Do you know how hard it is to knock someone out in a way that can't cause permanent damage, to knock someone down so they don't really fall down and get their clothes dirty?"

"Stop complaining," Frost said, waiting as Veronique opened the rear door on the passenger side, "and start undressing her—hurry up!"

Frost walked away, lighting a cigarette. After a while, the nurse would awaken, dressed in the black ninja outfit, loosely tied, loosely enough that in an hour or so she could get herself free. Hopefully, she'd never know what had become of her nurse's uniform. "Hank!"

Frost turned around, walking back toward the car, intentionally not looking into the rear seat. "What?"

"This woman—she is bigger than I am—much—I—"

"Take some of her underwear—stuff it into the bra—that should do it."

"I don't like doing that—it's—"

"Practical," Frost smiled into the darkness.

"You try wearing a bra that is four sizes too big for you, maybe five!"

"My heart bleeds," Frost said, then walked away again.

He was on his second cigarette when he heard Veronique call to him again. "Hank?"

He turned around, then saw her, standing a few feet behind him—the white dress, the white cap, the blue cape, the white shoes and stockings. "You look just like a real bonafide nurse, kid," he smiled, walking toward her, kissing her cheek.

"Fitting my hair under this damned cap took forever."

"Looks good," he smiled. "You got her tied up?"

"Yes—now what?"

"Well—you can get into the hospital—at least into the main part of the building disguised as a nurse. We gotta get me in. You're gonna use your karate to put a few highly visible but hopefully not too painful bruises on my face—then you walk me in. They must have an occasional mugging in a city this size, some street crime. On your way to work you found me wandering around in a daze and—"

"That is absurd—"

"It'll work—what? You think I like letting somebody pound lumps on me? You think of a better idea, I'll try it."

"Why don't we try to hijack an ambulance, pull up to the emergency room—I could bandage your face, I could—"

"Two reasons—three really," Frost told her patiently. "One: any security guy worth his pay is going to suspect somebody with his face covered with bandages; second: to do that we'd need three people, one of them to drive the ambulance. We don't have three people unless I missed something along the way. Third— ambulances usually have radios, so we'd have to get into guns and so far we haven't killed anybody that didn't need it and there's no sense starting.''

"I cannot do what you ask—it is—''

"You want me to stand here and start calling you every filthy name in the book until you lose your temper and slug me anyway, or what?''

"I can't!''

"You'd better—that nurse isn't going to stay out forever; we've got about thirty hours before the terrorist deadline—time's wasting. Hit me hard.''

"I can't!''

"In the face—so it shows good. Just don't screw up my teeth or break anything. Hit me!''

"I cannot, Hank! I don't want to hurt you, I—''

"I don't want to be hurt either—I'm no kink, but there's no other way. Now do it—and fast.''

She took a half step back, her left hand flashing upward, Frost exercising all the strength of his will not to sidestep, to block the blow, feeling the edge of her hand hammer against the right side of his face, starting to fall back under the blow but standing his ground. "Some more,'' he rasped, his face stinging, numbing.

Her right snapped up toward him, across his left cheek and down, the force of the blow snapping his head to the side. "Again—come on—get it over with,'' he rasped through his gritted teeth.

She hit him again, then again, numbness taking over his face, his head aching. Again, then she fell against him, crying and Frost held her in his arms, whispering to her, "It was something that had to be done, and you did it." He forced a laugh, saying, "I would have done the same for you."

She looked at him then and Frost could see there were tears in her eyes. "Your face—it is—"

"Just what we needed, kid."

He got her to help him rip the left sleeve of his windbreaker, then he rubbed the windbreaker along the alley floor, getting it dirt smeared and greasy.

"You look terrible," she smiled. "As though you'd been run over by an automobile."

"That's not bad then," Frost tried to smile, his face hurting. "I feel like I was run over by a truck. Let's go—I'll run the plays by you as we walk."

Frost's plan was simple—he hadn't had the time or the facts to lay out one that was more complex. Had he possessed the layout of the hospital, the schedules of the security police guarding the kneecapped journalist, or any other information, it would have been easier. But the time needed to acquire the information was the critical factor and there had been none of that. He trusted Karama, at least marginally, but getting Captain Karama to help him penetrate the hospital would have been useless. Karama would not have sanctioned what Frost planned to do, what Frost felt was the only way to get the injured journalist to tell what he knew about the hiding place where Marlene Staudenbruch was likely being held.

As they reached the hospital steps, Frost spotted the first of the guards. Already leaning heavily on the girl, he started to stumble, one of the guards

139

rushing down to them, speaking in Turkish. Veronique answered, in Turkish again. Frost imagined she was running the mugging story by the man. In an instant, the guard was supporting Frost under the right arm, Veronique under the left, the two of them almost carrying Frost toward the steps, then up and into the corridor toward the rear of the hospital. The sign in the corridor read in Turkish, French and English, "EMERGENCY TRAUMA CENTER."

There was a vacant wheelchair in the corridor and Frost, his good eye half-closed saw Veronique gesture toward it, heard her say something. The uniformed police guard reached out for the chair, Veronique supporting Frost a moment as the chair was unfolded, then both of them helping Frost into the chair. There was a hurried conversation between Veronique and the guard, Veronique smiling a lot, then pressing the young guard's hand for an instant. The guard bent toward Frost, said something totally incomprehensible to Frost and smiled, then walked briskly away.

Veronique was behind him, the chair already in motion. Frost heard her whisper, "What is the expression? So long, so well?"

"So far, so good," Frost corrected. "Keep rollin'—but don't get me into that emergency room."

Frost let his head loll forward, a nun passing them in the hall, stopping to look at him, crossing herself when Veronique spoke to her in Turkish again. The sister smiled, then started past them.

Frost's face hurt; Veronique despite her reluctance had done too good a job, he thought. He wondered if she'd cracked his left cheekbone. There was a stairwell entrance at the far end of the hall and Veronique stopped the chair beside it, tried the door, first feeling around it for alarm wires. Frost alternately watched her and watched the now empty corridor.

"Let's go," he rasped, pushing himself out of the chair and grasping the door handle—a panic lock—and shoving his way through, Veronique pushing the chair in behind him.

Frost glanced along the stairwell landing, then above and below. "I just wish to—"

"I learned where he was," the girl said.

"How?" Frost was startled.

"The young guard—I told him I was a specialty nurse in orthopedics assigned to assist with the unfortunate case of the journalist Mundafik. He asked me if I knew my way from the emergency room to the fourth floor."

Frost leaned toward her, kissing her on the cheek. "You're an angel."

"Your poor face," she almost cooed.

"You can kiss it and make it well later, huh," Frost smiled. "I'll be fine." He wasn't certain as he said it though. "Fourth floor—European style?"

"Oui—I think so."

"Okay," Frost said. "Give me my gun and the spare mags and stuff."

The French girl reached into the massive black purse she'd borrowed from the nurse along with the uniform, extracted the worn-blue High Power

141

and handed it to Frost. Frost snapped the slide back, chambering the first round, then raised the safety catch, pocketing the spare magazines and the loose ammo as well, making the gun disappear butt forward behind his right kidney under his tattered windbreaker. "Let's go," he rasped, starting up the steps two at a time, looking back once and seeing the girl behind him, the cape swaying around her as she walked, almost ran behind him. Fourth floor in Europe translated to fifth floor in America, he knew—meaning four double flights of steps. One more flight remained when he finally stopped, slightly out of breath, letting the girl catch him on the landing, putting his hands on her shoulders, saying to her, "We take out any guards as inconspicuously as possible—I'll need a couple of minutes with Mundafik."

"What are you going to do?"

"Put a gun to his head and convince him of my sincerity—"

"You would kill him?"

"No," Frost shrugged. "I'm a softy—but he doesn't know that. With this face, these clothes, the eyepatch, and the muzzle of this Browning all looking him in the eye he should pretty well take me for real."

"What if he is sedated?"

"Then we blew the ball game unless we can wake him up," Frost admitted. "Let's go."

More slowly now, to avoid telltale noise, he started up the last flight of stairs, stopping beside the door leading into the fourth floor corridor, his hand poised on the doorlock, his eye peering through the wire screened security window. He glanced behind him then, looking at the girl, whispering, "Ready?"

"Oui—yes. I like you—don't forget."

"Okay," he smiled, his face hurting when he did. "Me too."

Slowly, Frost applied pressure to the door handle, pulling it in toward him, cautiously stepping into the corridor.

He looked to his right. There was no one in sight. He looked to his left. In the same instant as he saw the guard, the guard turned his head toward Frost. Their eyes met. The guard didn't move. Frost smiled at the man, asking, "I bet you're wondering what I'm doing here?"

The Turkish police guard looked bewildered.

"Well—I have a really good explanation," Frost went on, smiling. "And I know you'd love to hear it. And I'd love to tell—"

The young man started for his gun and Frost lashed out with his right foot, supporting himself on the door handle, the toe of his foot connecting with the policeman's chest, knocking the man off the chair on which he sat, Frost diving after him, lacing him once across the jaw with his left fist. The policeman was out for the count.

Frost looked up, behind him. Veronique was standing there. "Help me move him into the stairwell," Frost ordered. He thought to himself that lately he couldn't seem to avoid breaking into hospitals and fighting policemen—it was a dangerous habit.

Frost dragged the man across the floor, putting

him behind the stairwell door and taking his gun, using his cuffs to secure him to the stair railing. He started back into the corridor again. This time there was no one.

It was a good sized hospital, Frost had determined, and there was no way of knowing exactly in which wing the kneecapped journalist was being treated. It was simply a matter of finding an aggregate of policemen and gravitating toward them. This he started to do. With no additional police guards in view, Frost decided the north wing of the hospital was definitely the wrong place, then started walking quickly along the corridor, trying to avoid a nursing station but almost stumbling on it at the end of the hall.

Two women were there, one of them apparently working at some paperwork, her eyes cast down behind the counter, but the second woman—as Frost watched from the corner of the hallway—was staring off into space, as if thinking. And she was staring his way. There was a door beside him and Frost cautiously opened it. Some sort of supply closet, he reasoned.

Cupping his hands to his lips, he whispered in Veronique's ear, "Leave your cape and purse with me—then go in about five or six of those rooms down there and push the nurse call buttons—should get both of them out of that nurse's station so we can get past."

She merely nodded, unbuttoning the collar of the cape and swinging it off her shoulders, handing Frost the cape and shoulder bag, then looking behind her and starting off. "I'll be in here," he rasped and she nodded again as he gestured toward the supply closet.

Frost stepped inside, waiting, the door ill fitted and with his eye pressed to it where it joined the doorframe by the hinges he could see a four foot section of the corridor. It seemed like an eternity to him, but faintly hearing buzzing sounds, he assumed from the nurse call switches, he began to hear the click of heels on the corridor floor, whispered, unintelligible conversation. One white-dressed figure moved past his field of vision, then a second. In a moment, the door started to open and Frost stepped back.

"Hank?"

"Let's go," he rasped, starting into the hallway, running behind Veronique past the now vacated nurses' station. They ran down the next corridor, toward the west wing, Frost running abreast of the girl now, reaching out to her left shoulder as he slowed, flattening himself beside her along the corridor wall. There were two guards posted outside a room at the far end of the hall. Unless there were more than one endangered VIP under care in the hospital, it had to be the room of Mundafik, the kneecapped journalist.

"What do we do, Hank?"

Frost looked at the girl a moment, then back toward the two guards. "A shootout would be pointless—all we'd do is get ourselves trapped here. Let's just walk up on the guards, and when I make my move we take 'em out, quick. Drag 'em into the room, you keep watch while I talk with Mundafik. Move out," he growled, starting to

145

walk down the hallway, trying to look casual, Veronique a few paces behind him. There was apparently a reasonable amount of traffic in the hospital corridor—the guards didn't look at all alarmed.

Frost passed the nearest of the two men, each flanking the door, then as Veronique came even with the first man whom Frost had passed, Frost jumped for the second man, his right fist hammering forward, catching the guard on the left side of the jaw. Frost's knuckles stung as the man slumped in his chair, starting to go down, but still, almost feebly, reaching for the pistol in the flap holster at his side. Frost's left hand locked on the man's gunhand wrist, Frost's right crossing the man's jaw again, catching it on the tip, the man's head snapping back.

Frost glanced to his right, having heard no sound there. Veronique stood there, her feet wide apart, looking as though she'd barely moved, the first guard in a heap on the floor in front of her, appearing to be asleep.

Frost grinned, shaking his head, then started to haul the second guard up under the armpits. "Take my gun and take the door," Frost commanded. He could feel the girl reaching under his tattered windbreaker, see the blue worn Browning High Power snake in her hand, toward the door. Her left hand reached out for the doorknob and she twisted it, pushing the door inward, then stepping in quickly, the pistol in both her hands now.

"It is all right, Hank," she said in a loud, stage whisper.

146

Frost began dragging the second guard through the opened doorway. "Heavier than he looks," Frost panted, dropping the man as gently as he could on the floor, then going for the other man. The guard Veronique had taken out was lighter, and more easily this time Frost dragged the unconscious body across the floor and into the hospital room.

"All right—wait by the door," Frost told her, Veronique slipping past him, her cape and shoulder bag over her left arm. Frost approached the bed, the man lying there seemingly asleep. There was an I.V. tube leading from his left forearm, some sort of tube out of the man's nose. The left leg was completely covered with a blanket, and seemed vastly larger than the right leg half exposed under the sheet. Frost approached the man, staring at him. Dark haired, dark circles around the eyes, a heavy, bushy mustache. Frost turned away, snatching the guns from the two unconscious guards lying there on the hospital room floor. He checked each, found them chamber loaded, then walked back to the bed, one of the little Turkish .32s in each fist.

Frost shook the man, gently by the shoulder, Mundafik moving but only slightly. He was banking on the man knowing English. "Mundafik—wake up. Hurry," Frost rasped. "Mundafik!"

The man's eyelids fluttered, then opened. His eyes were brown with green flecks in them, totally out of place for a Turk, Frost thought. He shrugged. "Mundafik—wake up. Come on!"

Frost shook the man's shoulders again, this time more violently.

"Engli—"

"Yeah—English. Speak English. Mundafik!"

"What is it that—" It seemed as though the words were a labor for the man. Frost didn't envy him the severity of the leg wound.

"Mundafik—wake up."

"What is it—who are—"

"My name doesn't matter—but these do," and Frost brought both pistols' muzzles up to the wounded journalist's eye level. And the eyes widened.

"What do you—"

"I want one thing, and one thing only. I'll ask it once. If you don't tell me what I want to know, I'll shoot both your eyes out and you'll be dead, here and now. Got it?"

The man just nodded, heavy beads of sweat forming on his forehead and his upper lip.

"I'm searching for the woman Marlene Staudenbruch—she was kidnapped by the right wing terrorist group of Colonel Dashafik and the left wing terrorists—The Popular Front for The Liberation of Fascist Europe—they kneecapped you. I want to know where Marlene Staudenbruch was taken. And before you answer me, I got into this hospital once, past all the guards, and I can do it again. If you lie, feed me the wrong information—anything; I'll get back," Frost lied. He had no intention of committing what to him would have been a cold blooded murder. Finding Bess if she were alive was his consuming passion, but

148

finding her and being someone totally different whom she wouldn't love and he wouldn't expect her to love would have been like not finding her at all. Something, something he couldn't really define and felt almost afraid of, was making him feel more and more that indeed she was somehow alive.

He levelled the identical .32 ACP pistols at the journalist, Mundafik. "Where is Marlene Staudenbruch?"

He waited, watching something strange in the journalist's eyes, watching the eyes as they seemed to brighten, watching the man's face seaming with laughter. "Go ahead. Those guards? They are a suicide watch. After this—" and Mundafik moved his left arm, his left hand gesturing toward the hidden leg, "do you think I want to live? Shoot me! Please! I'll tell you nothing—I want to die."

Frost looked at the man, feeling his own eye widen. He uttered, "My God . . ."

Chapter Seventeen

Frost could hear the clock ticking—it was somewhere in the room but he hadn't seen it. He could hear the slightly labored sound of Mundafik's breathing, he could hear his own pulse drumming in his ears. Bess—had to find her, had to know the truth. Staudenbruch—had to find her in order to know the truth. Veronique—if she waited much longer in the corridor outside the hospital room, she'd be discovered and in jeopardy, more so than she already was. And suddenly, Frost felt very angry, angry at himself and the world for the situation he was in, and angry at Mundafik. Suicide was something Frost could comprehend. You were being attacked by savages or terrorists and when they would swamp you, before they'd kill you, they'd mutilate you. Then you'd fight, until you'd killed everyone you could, until they were pulling you down. Then—maybe—the old last bullet routine, what they called the "dutch act."

Frost set the pistols down on the foot of the bed, then not looking at Mundafik, almost whispered, "My back's been so mutilated I thought I'd never walk—but I did, I do. This eye," and Frost raised the patch as he stared at the man across the hospital bed. "Anytime anybody ever asks me about it, how I lost it, and sometimes when I remember how I lost it, I feel like maybe I want to throw up, or find a hole and pull myself down into it and zip the ground closed over me. I make jokes about it. Yeah—you're probably gonna limp, you're probably gonna have a lot of pain, but you're alive. You're ahead of the game. I wasn't gonna murder you. That's not the way I am. Marlene Staudenbruch's people planted a bomb back in London several months ago. The woman I was going to marry was there, in the store that got blown all to hell. I thought she was dead, but then this friend of mine, he showed me this ring cops took off some West German terrorist.

"It was the ring she was wearing, the ring I'd given her! And dammit—I gotta know if she's alive! I gotta know!" He was shouting, standing, leaning over the bed, staring down at the man, Mundafik. "I gotta know!"

Frost turned away from the bed, walking toward the blind covered window.

"What is your name?"

"Hank Frost," the one-eyed man muttered, without looking back.

"Why do you tell me this?"

"I guess maybe sometimes it's good to know

other people got worse problems—maybe I just had to—"

"You love the woman you search for, yet to find her you must save a Communist terrorist."

"Communist terrorist, neo-Nazi terrorist, what the hell's the difference?" Frost asked. "All you guys seem bound and determined to screw up the whole world, knock people off whether they're involved with what you're fighting or not."

"What kind of man are you?"

"A soldier—I was, sometimes I still am. Soldiers don't—"

"Don't kill senselessly? I think they do."

Frost turned around, laughed and looked at Mundafik. "Yeah—but when you accidentally kill a civilian, kill a woman or a child, it doesn't make any difference to them, won't bring 'em back. You can't tell 'em you're sorry—none of that. But you didn't go out there that day to do that. You don't try to kill people who aren't part of the God damned game. Maybe we're just as bad—you, me, Marlene Staudenbruch. But I don't think so."

"You fight to make the world safe for democracy? You joke!"

"I fight to make the world safe for whatever it wants to be—just so it still has the right to choose. And that's not a joke."

"An idealist? Why aren't you a terrorist?"

"I guess I never figured I was so important that just because I wanted something to be a certain way, wanted it in my guts and felt it had to be that way—I guess I never figured that gave me the right to be a butcher."

152

"But surely—"

"What? The ends justify the means? You sound like Marlene Staudenbruch. I thought you were a right wing terrorist?"

"But that is not just a Communist slogan—the end does—"

"Some ends justify some means—any time you say all, all you do is turn off your mind, turn off your brain. You say—everythin's easy—I can do any of this terrible shit. It's okay to intentionally kill civilians, to murder priests and nuns, to blow up a synagogue, to snipe at policemen—that's okay because out of all this evil crap I'm doin', something good is gonna come from it. If you believe that, maybe you should commit suicide." Frost walked back to the bed, then handed the two pistols up from the bottom of the bed to Mundafik. The man wouldn't reach out and take them. Frost put the guns down hard on the man's abdomen, rasping, "Here—go shoot yourself. Then when your body's dead, it'll just match the rest of ya."

Frost turned away, starting toward the door. He stopped, cold, unmoving, hearing the journalist's voice, a strange quality in it, one Frost hadn't heard before. "In the highlands near the border, near the town of Edirne. Five miles southwest of the town is an old walled estate—it was owned by Colonel Dashafik's grandfather who fought in the Great War. It is a fortress. If she is anywhere, this Marlene Staudenbruch is there. But you will never get inside—it is impossible."

"Are you going to kill yourself—still?"

"No—I think I will not."

"Then I think I will get inside," Frost almost whispered, then added, "thank you." He opened the door and walked into the hallway, closing it behind him. As he leaned against the doorframe a moment, Veronique turned toward him. He watched her eyes a moment, then bent toward her face and kissed her cheek.

Chapter Eighteen

Frost considered hot-wiring a police car to have been very scientific. Veronique, beside him now as they left the car and walked along the rocky ground of the low hills, declared, "But the police will be able to follow the car—easily!"

"I sure hope so," Frost told her.

"I don't understand—but, you—"

"I don't have any reason to doubt Mundafik—if he says that place is a fortress, it probably is. And everyplace I've been, practically, the left wing terrorists have been right behind me. I don't have any reason to doubt they'll show up this time. Means we're going to be right in the middle of a little war with some pretty heavily armed people. And I don't think anybody's gonna care about keeping us alive—except us."

"Then if the police follow the car—"

"They'll wind up walking in on the right wing terrorist hideout, the left wing terrorists. Us too."

"A war—hmmm."

"A war," Frost told her. "By tonight," and Frost glanced up at the just rising moon. It would be full. "By tonight," he repeated, "there'll be a very bloody war, all over one lousy terrorist."

"You believe it is something different, n'es-ce pas?"

"Yes," Frost answered, climbing a rocky hillock and reaching back, helping the girl. She had changed out of the borrowed nurse's clothes and back into her own things, but the mid-calf length skirt she wore and the medium heeled boots were only marginally practical with the terrain. She stopped, standing beside him a moment, pushing her long, dark hair back from her face.

"What is the reason for all this, then?" she asked, sounding slightly breathless.

Frost lit a cigarette, started walking again, but more slowly, the girl beside him. "I've been running it through my head, over and over again. And there's only one thing that makes sense out of all of this. Let's say Marlene Staudenbruch didn't really want to defect at all. Let's say she was captured alive, by one of the intelligence agencies friendly with the CIA. Maybe the British, the West Germans, somebody like that. Then let's say some clever case officer in CIA told her that if she cooperated, she'd be given a new identity and a new lease on life, but if she didn't, they'd leak word she'd ratted on the terrorists and let her out on the street unprotected. She wouldn't have any choice if she wanted to keep breathing, right?"

"Oui—I think so . . ."

"Well. Let's say they came up with a wonderful

156

idea to get a net on a whole bunch of left wing and right wing terrorists.''

"A net?"

"Yeah—get 'em in the bag; capture them. It's perfect. They created a fictitious CIA terrorist plant, then they put out the story that Marlene was going to defect to the United States to reveal the name of this double agent. Now, since she was so high up in the Popular Front for The Liberation of Fascist Europe, her people couldn't be certain that there wasn't a CIA double she'd been using. You gotta remember her track record—one success after another, whether a bombing, a kidnapping, an assassination—whatever. Could have easily had wires into the CIA or some other big intelligence agency. Only makes sense. So now, when they put her on the run, her own people would be after her, whether they bought the CIA plant routine or not. But the right wing terrorists—the neo-Nazi tied in people—well, they could see a real advantage in grabbing Marlene. If they got her to spill who the CIA contact was, they could put wires on him themselves. Simply threaten the guy with exposure. That'd give them pre-emptive news of counter-terrorist measures taken by the various intelligence and police agencies in Europe and Asia Minor. And to run the operation—on both sides—it'd probably pull the big planners from both the right and left wing groups. Get all the fish together into one barrel. What better place than Turkey. A pro-American government, an active right wing terror group it wasn't too pleased about. The Turkish police and military intelligence people would have been more than happy to help out. Everybody would be happy."

"But what about Marlene Staudenbruch? Surely she would have—"

"Maybe she would have realized what they'd do to her, but I don't think they gave her the whole set-up. Back there in Italy when some of the left wing terrorists went after Marlene and me. Well, she was reluctant to shoot because she could get away and didn't want to kill her own people. In the hotel in Rome, she wasn't sure if they were right or left wing people, and anyway she was in imminent danger of getting shot herself. So she helped me out. On the train, she probably recognized one of the guys as being with the Colonel's group and opened up on them. I don't think they bothered mentioning to Marlene that they were going to let her sit with the right wing terrorist people. She might have started shooting to avoid someone shooting her, or because she lost her nerve, maybe was going to double-cross the CIA. I don't know. But they're letting her sit while they wait for the left wing people to get on line. Catch everybody at once. They might not know exactly where the Colonel's people would have put her, anyway. So there's old Marlene, thumb screws in place, the whole nine yards, lying her head off."

"Lying?"

"Yeah—to keep them torturing her and keep them from killing her. She's on the hot seat but good. If I were cruel, I'd say it couldn't happen to a nicer girl."

"But why did they involve you?"

"I involved myself. My buddy O'Hara got me the job, and the CIA people grabbed me like I was the best thing they'd ever seen. What's better to make a defecting terrorist more noticeable to the people you want to kidnap her than a one-eyed man? I couldn't disguise myself if I tried. And I guess I've got a reputation for staying power. The Company probably figured I'd take care of any of the left wing people who tried killing her, or at least die trying, cover her to keep on the route until the snatch could be made."

"But the men on the train?" Veronique said, taking Frost's cigarette, dragging heavily on it.

"I don't know who they were. If they were so eager to knock me off, I'd bet they were from the Colonel's group, but I'll never know for sure."

"Then," and she stopped, turned around and stared up at him. "Then we not only walk into a battle, we walk into a deathtrap."

"A killing ground—better expression, more apt. A killing ground. All that's waiting is for all the participants to show up before the shooting starts."

"And you go there to find out about the woman—about Bess?"

"That's why I go."

"You love her a great deal—I envy her," Veronique almost whispered.

"But there's no reason for you to go on," Frost told her.

"I will go—if you learn your Bess is still alive, you'll need help getting out. And if you learn she

159

is dead, you'll need help wanting to get out. I will go.''

"What if I don't let you?" Frost asked her.

"Shoot me? Hardly. And I fight better than you even if I am a woman."

Frost tried to smile, then felt the soreness and stiffness in his face where he had made her hit him so they could get into the hospital.

He rubbed his left cheek, still wondering if she'd given him a hairline fracture there. "A telling argument. I can't stop you. All right."

He started walking again. The brightness of the moon was not to his liking. Apparently no one who'd set this thing up had thought about the old line, "Dark of the moon." It would be a perfect night for shooting fish in a barrel, he thought.

Chapter Nineteen

The moon was high overhead, bathing the fortified house in light so bright Frost could have almost read to pass the time. But he was too busy to read. The thought had crossed his mind that perhaps Veronique had been in on it all along, been on the train not to find the runaway Marlene Staudenbruch, but to inform the right wing terrorists, or the CIA, or somebody, on Frost's progress with the Staudenbruch woman. But Frost had summarily dismissed the idea. If Veronique had been there to spy, she'd proven her good intentions since then, saving his life, helping him. Frost thought it odd about himself, that he rarely carried a grudge. He decided, laughing at himself then, that it was all part of what he labeled his inherent dopiness—letting people take advantage of him, set him up, run him through the treadmill, the maze. He was tired of it, but he'd known men who'd never trusted anyone, never stopped to believe in anything. Frost had subconsciously decided long years back that believing in something was all that made you alive.

He turned to the girl beside him. "Veronique?"

"Oui?"

"Give me a kiss—now," and the girl leaned toward him, Frost's hands touching her face, his mouth touching hers.

"Why did you do that?"

"Because it's time to go, I think. There's been some movement on the far side of the ridge—over there," and Frost pointed beyond the fortified stone house. "If I were running this, I'd probably attack right now. The moon is as bright as ever, and no sensible person would expect an attack now. So it's the best time to attack, coming up along that ridge, out of sight until the last hundred yards to the house. I think it's going to be now. We have to go when it starts."

"Is that why you chose this place—there is an open area of perhaps three hundred yards to cross—"

"If an attack comes, it'll come on the least exposed side, so when it comes all the defending fire will be concentrated there. We should get to the wall okay."

"I like you—remember that," she whispered, kissing his cheek.

The one-eyed man smiled at her, squeezed her hands a moment in his, then snatched the worn blue Browning High Power from his belt. "Ready?"

"I am ready," she whispered back. The two .38 Special revolvers she'd taken from the left wing terrorist stronghold were in her hands now, one a vintage Colt Official Police, the other a Smith & Wesson heavy barrelled Military and Police model. There had been no way to take the Sten guns the terrorists had used, although now Frost wished he had.

Frost looked across the rocky hillside, toward the far ridgeline, detecting some faint movement there again. He glanced at the face of the Rolex on his left wrist. "Bess . . ." he murmured. His eye riveted on a shadow on the far side of the stone wall surrounding the house—a man? He strained to see more clearly. A man, yes. "They're coming," Frost whispered to Veronique.

"Hank?"

"Yes," he answered, still studying the far ridgeline.

"I stopped just liking you—I love you."

He looked at her, studied her eyes, then took her right hand in his, taking the revolver from it, touching his lips to it. "That's what you're supposed to do, isn't it—with a French girl? Kiss her hand?"

She started to answer him, but then Frost turned away—there was a long burst of automatic weapons fire from the wall surrounding the house on the ridgeline side. He could see the flash. "Let's go," he snapped, pushing himself up to his feet, the Browning pistol back in his right hand, his thumb wiping down the safety lever. There was no sound but the crunch of small rocks under his feet as he ran, and the sound of his own breathing in his ears. He glanced behind him once. Her skirt

163

hitched up in her left hand, one of the revolvers in her waistband, Veronique was running after him, the second revolver clenched tight in her tiny right fist.

He looked forward again, toward the house, hearing another burst of automatic weapons fire from the ridgeline side of the wall. He glanced skyward—the moon was a glaring white disk and the sky itself was cloudless, seeming to glow with the moonlight. There was more gunfire, coming now from both the wall and the ridgeline itself.

Frost started running faster, knowing now that it was a matter of time until someone from the wall saw them, thinking they were part of the attacking left wing terrorists, or someone from the ridgeline, thinking they were right wing terrorists trying to reach the safety of the fortified stone house.

More gunfire, the ground beside Frost's running feet chewing up with it. "Keep running, Veronique," he shouted, snaking the cocked Browning High Power toward the source of the gunfire—the ridgeline—and firing two wild shots. There was gunfire pouring down on them from the wall now and Frost pointed the muzzle of the High Power toward the top of the wall, swinging the gun to rest in the palm of his left hand and snapping off two, two-round bursts. He heard a faint groaning sound, a smile crossing his lips as he ran on. The wall was less than a hundred yards ahead now.

"What do we do when we get there?" It was Veronique screaming behind him.

"Improvise!" Frost shouted, still running. There was more gunfire now, but from the ridgeline only—they were too close to the wall for the men defending the far side to get them into their sights.

The rough looking stone wall was less than fifty yards off now, Frost bending low in an all out dead run for it. The one-eyed man lobbed two more shots toward the ridgeline, answering a long, largely inaccurate automatic weapons burst, the ground six feet away from him erupting under the impact of the assault rifle bullets.

He reached the wall, almost hurling himself against it, waving his left hand frantically to the girl, "Come on—run for it!"

She was running, hard, still fifteen yards back. There was a burst of gunfire from the ridgeline, a tiny scream, almost inaudible over the gunfire, and she went down.

Frost felt the muscles around his eye tense, the cords in his neck go taut. He raced away from the wall, toward the girl, scooping her up into his arms and running with her, the ground around his feet tearing under the impact of assault rifle fire.

He reached the wall, sinking with his back against it to the ground, the girl still in his arms. Her eyelids fluttered, then opened. He looked away from her face to a ragged splotch of red on the left sleeve of the gray silk blouse she wore. He missed his Gerber knife then, instead taking the little knife from his money clip and cutting at the sleeve, then ripping it down, letting it dangle from her wrist.

"Like they say in the movies, kid—a flesh wound. You were lucky. Could've had your arm torn off."

"I can make it—I fainted when I was hit—the pain of it—I don't—"

"I know you can make it," Frost told her, sitting her up on the ground beside him, ripping the sleeve away from her wrist. "I can't leave you here. I'll bandage this to check the bleeding. Might hurt," and Frost, after probing the wound as gently as he could, knotted the sleeve twice at its center to pack as much of the fabric over the grazing wound as he could, then tied the sleeve bandage around her arm just below the shoulder. "Bullet didn't penetrate—you should be fine. Maybe a scar. Can you walk?"

Frost got to his feet, shifting the High Power into his left hand, searching for a spare magazine, then dumping the partially spent magazine and replacing it with a full one. "Can you walk?" he repeated, helping the girl to a standing position against the wall beside him.

"Yes—slowly a little while, but—"

"Okay—you're a tough kid. You never let go of your revolver—I bet you don't even remember it." He looked down at her right hand a moment. She smiled thinly at him. "Come on—hug the wall as much as you can. Let's go."

Frost started forward. There was a service gate, small, just large enough for a small truck or wagon to go through and he was heading for it—his best means over the wall. He glanced upward—twelve feet of stone and masonry, rough stone, the kind he could climb if he had to, but too difficult for the girl now that she was wounded.

The gunfire was heavier now, an occasional stray burst coming toward them from the now visible attackers along the ridgeline. He could see ragged groups of running figures working toward the far side of the wall, their weapons' muzzle flashes bright against the shadows formed by the moonlight on the rocks and the wall itself. They'd be coming over the wall soon, Frost realized, and he had to beat them inside.

"The Colonel's guys—they're going to be sending someone along here, to get us. Watch it, kid," he said over his shoulder. Frost glanced back at her—she looked weak, but was moving, her skin perhaps paler seeming than it had been, but her eyes were bright in the moonlight. "We'll make it," he told her reassuringly, but not half believing it.

The gate in the wall—the chink in the wall, he hoped—was another ten yards ahead; he could see its darkness set against the grayness of the wall. There was a noise from above and something—Frost didn't know what—made him step away from the wall, bringing the muzzle of the Browning up. A man—the profile of an assault rifle silhouetted against the moonlight. Frost fired twice, the Browning bucking in his hands harder than it would have because of the way he held his wrists, the hot brass searing his battered face. The assault rifle spit fire once, then the man tumbled off the wall, Frost sidestepping as the body crashed down toward him. "Good deal," Frost rasped, bending down to the man—if the bullets hadn't killed him, there was a broken neck from the fall. Frost pried the assault rifle—a beat up AK-47—from the dead fingers, then grabbed the three magazines stuffed in the man's belt.

Frost moved back toward the wall. "There'll be another one," he rasped, checking the action on the AK-47, setting it to full auto, ramming the spare magazines for it in his own belt. "Come on; the gate's up ahead." Frost moved out along the wall again, the AK-47 in his right fist, the High Power in his left.

He could see the gate clearly now, less than six feet away. There was a burst of gunfire from overhead, the ground by Frost's feet ripping under its impact. The one-eyed man rolled out away from the wall, the Browning and the AK-47 opening up toward the top of the wall. Two men, assault rifles blazing, swung toward him, the AK-47 bucking hard in Frost's right hand, the stock locked with his elbow against his right side. Frost felt something tearing at his left leg, his knee buckling, his left hand with the Browning still in it going up to his face as he tumbled forward.

There was a groaning sound, then a long burst of automatic weapons fire as Frost looked up. One of the two men was gone from the wall. The second man was shouldering his assault rifle, Frost trying to bring the AK-47 he held up on target. Suddenly, out of the corner of his eye, Frost could see a figure moving, heard Veronique's voice. "Pig—over here!"

The man hesitated an instant, Frost getting the muzzle of the AK-47 up, but hearing a single shot from his left. He glanced toward the origin of the sound. Veronique held the big old Colt revolver in her right fist, her arm extended. There was a thudding sound and Frost, on his feet, wheeled,

168

the second man falling heavily to the rocky ground.

"Got yourself an assault rifle, sweetheart," Frost rasped. He limped toward the dead man, bending down for the gun—another AK-47. The man's coat pockets bulged and Frost quickly searched them, finding one magazine each in the inside breast pockets. Limping back toward the wall, he handed the girl the rifle. "Can you handle it with your arm like that?"

The girl moved her left arm, her face, half in shadow from the wall, registering pain. "Oui—your leg?"

"I've been shot worse, kid," he smiled. He dumped the partially spent magazine from the AK and replaced it with a full one from his belt, stuffing the other magazine in his hip pocket.

"I know," she smiled. "Let's go—oui?"

"Yes," he smiled, turning toward the gate. The gunfire from the far side of the wall was more intense now, and closer to the ridgeline as they were, there was sporadic fire from there reaching near them, a burst hammering into the wall a few feet from his head as he ducked, rock chips pummeling his beaten face.

Forst's teeth gritted, his lips drawn back. He started for the gate, finding a ledge of support timber, the AK slung from his shoulder. "Cover me," he snapped to the girl. His left thigh burned as he moved his leg, but he focused on his hands, on finding a purchase on the gate for them, on pulling his body up with them, then reaching again for the top of the gate itself.

Frost peered over the gate, seeing running men at the far end of a long, narrow courtyard by the far wall. "Be back," Frost snapped, swinging his right leg over the top of the rough wooden gate, his left hand catching on a sliver of wood, starting to bleed. He dragged his left leg over the gate top, then half fell, half jumped to the rocky ground of the courtyard. "Aagh!" he screamed, coming down too hard on the wounded leg. His right eye was tearing with pain as he pushed himself up, half stumbling toward the gate. There was a heavy padlock—something from another era—binding a chain to the two sides of the gate, locking it, then a crossbar over and above it. "Stay away from the gate," Frost shouted, hoping Veronique had heard him.

The AK-47 was under his right arm now, on its sling. He shifted it forward, moving the selector off safe to full auto, stepping back a pace, then firing toward the lock, turning his face away as the half-rusted metal exploded under the impact of the jacketted slugs.

He moved back toward the gate, the wooden buttstock of the AK in his hands, hammering at the broken lock. He knocked it to the dirt, then pried at the chain. It was rusted in place. He hammered at it with the stock of the AK, the stock chipping, but the chain moving. He started to move the crosspiece, then heard the gravel crunching behind him. Frost fell back, rolling, the AK-47 swinging on line, his fingers fumbling the selector again to full auto. Two men—one with a stubby barrelled submachinegun, the nearest one

170

starting to fire. Frost fired first, a long, ragged burst. The man with the assault rifle rolled back, falling toward the second man, the submachinegun in the second man's hands ripping into the dirt beside Frost's leg as Frost fired again.

The subgunner stumbled, seemed to whirl like a dancer on his toes, then fell forward like a felled tree. Frost pushed himself to his feet, turning back to the gate, pushing at the crossbar. The wood was rotted, breaking under his hands as he lifted it away, then tugged at the gate.

It budged, creaking, the hinges, massive and rusted over, squeaking under the strain. The gate opened less than a foot; the girl was already starting through.

He leaned back, heavily against the wall, sighing. "Hi," he rasped.

"Here," the girl snapped, turning away from him, running toward the dead man with the subgun. In a moment she was back, handing Frost the submachinegun and three extra magazines. "Better, I think."

Frost nodded; the loss of blood in his leg—the pain . . . he pushed himself away from the wall, slinging the AK-47 across his back, checking the vintage German MP-40 the girl had taken from the dead man. "Looks like these guys robbed a museum," Frost smiled. He dumped the magazine, worked the bolt a few times, then replaced the magazine, the bolt locked open. "Let's hit the house," he told her, his left leg burning as he started to walk. But the girl was beside him, pulling his left arm across her shoulders. The one-eyed man stopped a moment, looking at her. "Okay," he murmured, then limped on.

Chapter Twenty

Frost had used the MP-40 "Schmeisser" once only, the 9mm subgun almost decapitating a man running out of the shadows by the kitchen doorway of the house. But Frost doubted the shots had been heard—the din of gunfire from the far wall was almost deafeningly loud now, sporadic bursts of gunfire from the courtyard around them. Frost imagined some of the left wing terrorists were coming over the wall. Time was against him.

The wooden stock of the AK-47 all but shattered as Frost knocked out the lock on the massive wooden door leading into the kitchen; yellow light glowed from a fire in the hearth, visible through the smallish, high windows. Throwing his left shoulder against the door, the door half fell off its hinges, inward, Frost narrowly keeping his balance. The subgun was in an assault position at his right hip. He limped through the doorway and across the stone floor, half stumbling over an overturned chair barely visible in the hearth light.

"Where would they keep her?" Veronique asked from behind him.

"Old place like this—probably a kind of half basement, like a root cellar. Maybe we can get to it through here," Frost answered, starting toward a door on the far wall of the huge room. The hinges looked almost polished with use. If it was a root cellar, Frost thought—he stopped, seeing a shining padlock on the door attached to a massive hasp. "This is it—gotta be," he called to the girl. She was beside him in a moment. Frost glanced around the kitchen. "Cover me while I go in—nobody down there but her, probably. Get up there, over by those cabinets; you can watch the outside door and the doorway into the rest of the house."

"All right!"

Frost looked around the doorframe, wanting to find a key. He'd smashed enough locks for the night. With his still bleeding left hand, he felt along the top of the doorframe. Nothing. He looked at his fingers. There was no dust either. He felt along the top of the frame again, feeling something small, cold and metallic under his fingertips.

The key. He placed it in the bottom of the padlock, twisted it and the lock sprung. He took the lock off the hasp, closing it and pocketing the key, then worked the hasp. The door would swing toward him. In case there were someone with the girl there, a last ditch guard, Frost wanted the door to open into the root cellar. He shrugged, then pulled on the door, stepping back. Nothing greeted him but darkness.

He glanced around the kitchen again; the small refrigerator was connected to a gas tank and he saw no evidence of electric light. There was a lantern on the rough hewn table at the center of the kitchen and he went to it, fumbling up the glass chimney, then working the striking wheel of his Zippo under his left thumb, lighting it, then lighting the lantern's wick. He burned the tips of his fingers, then lowered the glass chimney as he cursed softly under his breath.

"Wish me luck," he rasped to the girl, Veronique. He could barely see her behind the cabinets, the muzzle of the AK-47 stuck out ahead of her.

"Merde—some of us say that. Like the American expression—break an arm."

"It's leg," he grunted, staring back toward the root cellar door, the lantern in his left hand, the Schmeisser in his right.

There was a long row of uneven and ancient looking wooden steps just starting ahead of him. Hugging the stone wall—it was damp feeling when his hand rubbed against it—he started down, keeping the lantern away from his body, like a policeman with a flashlight entering an alley—make the light a target but away from you.

The steps creaked under his feet, one of them breaking as he put his weight on it. The one-eyed man stepped back, then cautiously stepped over it. If anyone were waiting, they would know he was coming, Frost rationalized. "Marlene!" He said it louder. "Marlene?"

There was a cry from the darkness—more

174

animal than human, half mingled he thought with a sob. "Frost!"

Swallowing hard, he reached the bottom of the steps, the yellow light casting about him, ahead of him on the wall at the far end of the cellar. He looked away, closing his eye, murmuring, "Holy God . . ."

Chapter Twenty-One

Frost walked slowly toward the far wall, keeping the lantern's light on his feet, not wanting to see what was ahead in the darkness. He could hear the voice though, still part human. "Kill me, Frost—kill me now. Don't look at me. Kill me."

"I'm sorry." He whispered the words, thinking they were stupid, but not thinking of anything better to say. He needed words, to remind him of the humanity of the thing, for the glimpse he'd gotten had been less than human.

He flashed the light on her again, the woman—what had been a woman—squinting her eyes tight against it, shrieking, "Kill me!"

It hardly seemed they'd forgotten a single element of torture, Frost thought. Burning—her hair had been burned from her head, huge blisters, oozing on the side of her face—what had been a face. Beating—her nose was gone—perhaps that was why the voice sounded as it did, the nose beaten to where it was a bumpy bloody mass on her face, half against

176

her left cheek. There was skin peeled from her breasts, from her abdomen; there were strangulation marks around her neck, as though they'd hung her by her neck for a time, trying to threaten her with death. But she'd had the classic misfortune of the captured man or woman with no information—no lie had sounded as convincing as the truth which she didn't know. Her hands were shackled by the wrists to the wall, but her left arm was clearly broken. He wondered she hadn't died of shock. But there were bruises along her arms and neck—needle marks, he supposed, drugs to keep her from dying. Her left foot was crudely bandaged and darkly stained. He didn't want to know what had been done to it. She opened her mouth to speak, the lips cracked and bloody, most of her teeth broken or altogether gone.

"I wouldn't try to force you. I can only ask, then I'll do as you asked me—kill you. I had nothing to do with this. I'll get as many of them as I can for you. But that bombing in London—the department store bombing I mentioned on the train I think it was. A woman—a woman I loved, she was in the store. I'd given her a ring. If she'd died, it would have been impossible—at least I think—impossible for the ring to have turned up on that dead West German terrorist. But it did. I gotta—"

The voice was hard to hear, the sound still only half human. "Put the light away from me."

Frost moved the lantern. "The man who died—you knew—"

"He slept with Carlotta Fleisch—all the time. She gave him the ring. I was there when she did it. She

177

laughed—saying it was so ugly it was beautiful. I don't know where she got it. Now kill me."

"Where's Carlotta Fleisch—please?" Frost asked.

"Scotland—I think. Scotland—yes, yes. I don't know anymore. Kill me now—please . . ."

Frost's throat was tight. "All right." He raised the lantern, then the muzzle of the Schmeisser. But the face that he saw made him lower the light. The eyes stared into the light, not squinting. The throbbing pulse visible seconds earlier in her neck had ceased. She was dead.

He wanted to cut her down—not wanting to but feeling he must. But the chains were forged together, not locked. The light now showed the anvil in the far corner of the cell and the cold forge behind it. "Calculated hopelessness," he whispered to himself in the darkness. If chains were locked to you, you could always hold the hope of somehow getting the key, or the rescuer finding it. There had been no hope of that for Marlene Staudenbruch. He suddenly noticed the smell—he knew what it was from as he turned away, following the lantern light back toward the steps, then up toward the top and the door into the kitchen. He reached the top of the steps, then stopped. He could hear the gunfire, louder now, as if some of the shooting were in the house itself.

"Hank? Was she—"

"You don't want to know. Yeah—she was. Don't ask me. She's dead—"

"Did—"

"No—she wanted me to. But she died there just now."

"Bess?"

"Maybe—another lead. Carlotta Fleisch. West German terrorist in Scotland maybe. Gotta find her. I'm gonna burn this place down and kill everybody I see here except you," Frost murmured.

"Burn—but—"

"A stone house'll burn—look at all the ceiling timbers, the roof, the furniture. It'll burn. We can get them all, maybe." Frost walked across the kitchen. There was a spinning wheel there, and beside it rough wooden boxes, some filled with thread, others with fiber. The fiber had the consistency of cotton batting. Frost took one of the boxes of the fiber and threw the contents across the oval braided rug covering part of the floor. "Help me—we'll go out the way we came in."

The girl was beside him then, moving another of the boxes as Frost took several handfuls of the fibers and carried them to the glowing hearth at the far end of the room, dragging the end of the oval rug after him. He stuffed the end of the rug up onto the coals then threw the fiber on the coals. The fiber smoldered a moment, then caught, the rug starting to catch. Frost started fast across the kitchen, toward the courtyard door, pushing Veronique ahead of him. He threw the lantern down in the largest of the boxes of fiber, the dry, ancient fiber catching, the coal oil from the lantern spilling across it, bursting into flames.

Frost pushed through the doorway, then levelled the subgun at the windows, firing it. "Air— needs more air," he murmured. He'd forgotten the pain in his left leg, forgotten it until he started

179

to back away, the pain returning, feeling the girl at his left side, supporting him.

"Hank—we have to get out of—"

"Wait," he whispered.

He could hear screams, cries—some of the gunfire seeming to ebb as the roof above the kitchen caught, an updraft starting with the heat, the flames leaping to eat the old, dry timbers, seeming to Frost to burn at the roof because the stone walls were denied them.

There was gunfire coming from his right and Frost turned, facing it. Men—some women—were running toward him, submachineguns and assault rifles in their hands, spitting tongues of flame. He stepped close to the stone wall, dropping behind it, then shouting to Veronique, "Keep down."

They were still coming as Frost snaked the muzzle of the Schmiesser around the corner of the squared off well. He didn't know if they were right wing terrorists or left wing. He decided there wasn't really a difference anyway. He started to fire, the Schmiesser bucking slightly in his hands, some of the terrorists in the lead going down. From beside him, he could hear the heavier chatter of Veronique's liberated assault rifle, more of the men and women charging toward the wall going down.

The Schmiesser was empty. Frost started firing his AK-47, emptied it then loaded a fresh magazine in both weapons. The house was a seething inferno now, the heat of the flames twenty yards distant searing Frost's face and hands as he watched, then fired again toward the attackers.

The AK was empty and he loaded it with the last full magazine, firing the Schmiesser then. There were a dozen of them coming and more behind them. Frost wondered if he'd make it out to find Carlotta Fleisch.

He started to shout something to Veronique but stopped; the gunfire momentarily stopped too. He looked upward, toward the moon and across it. Still at a distance, he could see a ragged line, the line looming larger and larger.

"Captain Karama's men," he smiled.

The attackers were already fleeing as Frost got to his feet, leaning against the well with the pain in his leg. The Schemisser in his right fist, the Browning was in his left. He fired and fired, feeling the brass pelting at him, the heat of it, the flames flickering across the ground as the house seemed to roar and groan.

Frost stopped shooting then, realizing finally the bulk of the attackers were out of range, letting the guns hang at his sides as he leaned against the well.

He could hear the helicopters now, hear the machinegun fire coming from them.

"Do you feel better, cheri?"

Frost looked over his shoulder at Veronique. "No—not a damn bit, not a bit." He closed his eye.

Chapter Twenty-Two

Frost limped on his cane—he resented canes—across the stone courtyard and toward the three small steps. There was a sidewalk restaurant a few paces beyond the stone steps and the previous day he had also gone there, the sun warm on his bruised face. Five days had passed, and Veronique had promised that this would be the last of the details she would have to work out with the police. Frost dismissed the thought then. He was tired from the exertion of the walk, too tired still from the loss of blood to leave Turkey for Scotland and to pursue the lead of Carlotta Fleisch. The doctors had told him it would be two more weeks. Frost judged another five days would do it. But the important factor of clearance from the Turkish authorities was still lacking. He had been ordered not to attempt to leave Istanbul.

By all accounts, he thought, navigating the first of the three stone steps, the operation had been a total success. Not so for Marlene Staudenbruch, but she was a terrorist, a murderess as Captain Karama had reminded him. Frost still felt it was a rotten way to go, but no one seemed interested in his opinion. Frost had made love with Veronique several times in the intervening days and what they felt, what they had done—despite his bad leg—had gotten better, better for them both, he thought.

He glanced down to the black face of the Rolex on his left wrist. In a few moments, Veronique would meet him.

Frost stopped at the last step, thinking perhaps he was getting old, but then reminding himself it was only the leg wound. It had been a bleeder. He walked the few paces to the nearest of the empty tables, sitting down heavily, getting the weight from his left leg. He fumbled in his pockets for a cigarette, the back of his left hand bandaged where he'd cut it going over the gate. Colonel Dashafik and several dozen of his men had died along with three dozen left wing terrorists—give or take, Frost thought. A successful operation—and for him as well, unless Marlene Staudenbruch had lied, made up a name just to get him to agree to kill her. He didn't think so. As he lit the Camel in the blue-yellow flame of his battered Zippo, he thought back to the moment he'd raised the muzzle of the Schmiesser, ready to put her out of her misery. But mercifully in the intervening seconds she had died.

"Coffee again, sir?"

Frost looked up at the waiter, answering, "Like I said yesterday—unless you got something stronger."

The man only smiled, walking away. Frost decided he should compliment the man on his English—it was very good.

"Hank!"

Frost looked up from studying the tip of his cigarette, saw Veronique running across the square, the sling holding her left arm looking somehow incongruous with the white summer dress she wore.

"Hi!"

"Hank," she sighed, out of breath, standing beside the table. He started to get up and she smiled, again breathlessly saying, "Hank—sit down. Here—" He watched her as she sat beside him, sweeping her skirt under her, then fumbling in the small handbag she carried for her cigarettes. Frost lit one for her—a DuMaurier.

"Are the cops finished with us?" he asked. He caught the eye of the waiter and signaled with two fingers, the man nodding. Frost looked back at her. "Are they finished?"

"Oui—yes. That is not the news, though. I made a few inquiries. But I don't see how you can go. But I learned—" And then she stopped.

"Learned what?" Frost asked, realizing he was holding her right forearm in a death grip.

"Learned something about the whereabouts of Carlotta Fleisch, Hank. Where she is in Scotland. The police there have her under surveillance. A house. A bomb factory they think. Something to do with submarine fences—"

"Submarine pens," Frost corrected absently.

"Oui—pens. But the police—I think from what

I learned they plan to raid the house by tomorrow night.''

"She'll be killed."

"Oui—I think so."

"I gotta get there."

"Are you tired, Hank—I—" She looked away from him, her long lashes the focus of his attention. She brushed a wisp of hair back from her face.

"I'd like to, too," Frost whispered.

"Will I see you again?"

"You don't lie, remember? I won't either."

"I still love you," she whispered.

"I know that," he answered.

"If you do not find Bess?"

"I don't know."

"I understand . . . Let us forget about tonight—you must leave soon but there is time. If you like," and she looked across the short expanse of table separating them.

The waiter came with the coffee, the small cups still seeming ludicrous to Frost.

"Very much," Frost told her.

He watched her green eyes, feeling the cigarette burn down to his fingers. "Incredible," he said half-aloud, watching her face.

Chapter Twenty-Three

"Captain Frost?" The man shouted over the engine noise of the military jet as Frost stepped down the laddered gangplank, the shock of the cold Scottish air assailing him through the raincoat he wore.

Frost, watching his breath steam, studied the florid-faced man a moment. "Yes—Inspector Thurmond?"

"Right you are, Captain. Good flight?"

"Not really," Frost shouted back, the Scottish policeman just laughing. Frost followed the man, a uniformed officer running past them both. Frost glanced behind him. The policeman was taking Frost's luggage from aboard the plane. His leg was stiff—from the protracted sitting aboard the four seater Grumann EA-6B Prowler, Frost had decided.

Frost leaned on the cane now as he stood beside the black Jaguar sedan, waiting while Thurmond conversed with another plain-clothes officer. Then

Thurmond turned toward Frost, smiling again, still shouting over the roar and whine of jet engines. "I have been told that for some reason we're to allow you into the house where Carlotta Fleisch and her terrorist friends have their little bomb factory. Something with your American CIA and all that?"

"Yeah—in a manner of speaking. I guess it was set up through them, and through Interpol," Frost answered.

"They'll kill you—I think they know they're under surveillance, probably have all their bombs ready to go when we attack. We've evacuated the entire area. But it won't really do us any good. We'll attack, they'll blow it up; a lot of our chaps will be killed. For what, eh?"

"You gotta—they gotta."

"Well put, sir—but why is it that 'you gotta', as you say?"

"Carlotta Fleisch has some information for me—at least I hope she does."

"But what good will it do for you to even get your information if you die?"

"I don't intend to die," Frost smiled. "I might freeze to death out here though."

"Ooh, quite—warmer climate, the change and all—sorry, dear boy—yes." Thurmond signalled the young uniformed officer to open the rear passenger door and gestured for Frost to get inside ahead of him. Frost slid across the seat, stretching his left leg as best he could while Thurmond slid in beside him. The door closed, the uniformed officer climbed into the front seat and started the engine. "I have a package for you—and a receipt for you to sign."

Frost took the brown cardboard box, then the felt tip pen the policeman offered and signed the bottom of the pink receipt form. Handing back the pen and the receipt, Frost opened the box. Wrapped in a copy of a Venice newspaper was his Metalife Custom Special, the speedloaders and his loose ammunition.

"Came through via diplomatic pouch, I understand," the police inspector volunteered.

"I didn't think you could have these over here," Frost smiled, checking the cylinder, loading the customized .357, then stuffing it back into the Bianchi Pistol Pocket inside holster. He dropped gun and holster in the pocket of his raincoat, the speedloaders and loose ammo going into his jacket pockets.

"I think if you have a penchant for guns, you'll be heartened to know that our Flying Squad chaps are quite expert in their use. Think you might be better off with a submachinegun than just a revolver. That's a customized Smith & Wesson, isn't it?"

"Yes," Frost murmured. He reached back into his raincoat, took the revolver and emptied the cylinder, then with the cylinder still open passed the gun over to Inspector Thurmond.

As Thurmond checked the gun, inspecting seemingly every detail while Frost watched, Thurmond began to speak, as if to the gun, not looking at Frost's face. "They're deadly people, Captain Frost—Carlotta Fleisch and her gang. We've reason to suspect the purpose of the bomb factory was twofold. You may have been briefed, and if I go over old ground, forgive me. But aside from making bombs which the IRA plants, they have apparently been making some sort of explosive device to use at the submarine base at Holy Loch. Nuclear submarines there—could be very nasty business if they got a bomb in there. What you might call desperate characters."

"I'll be careful," Frost said dutifully.

"Why—I mean if it isn't hush-hush—What's the reason for this precious ten minutes of yours, to get in and find this Carlotta Fleisch?"

"It's no big secret," Frost answered, looking out the window at the scattered lights in the misty darkness. "Carlotta Fleisch gave her boyfriend a ring, and he was found with it when the West German police nailed him in a robbery. The ring was one I'd given a woman named Bess Stallman—an engagement ring. I gave it to her the last time I saw her alive. She was in a department store in London when it was bombed and—"

"The bombing at—"

"Yes," Frost continued. "If she died in the bombing and if like a lot of the others they never could find the body, then the ring should be lost too. Here's the ring," and Frost opened the worn velvet box carried in his pocket.

Inspector Thurmond said, "May I?"

Frost only nodded, the Inspector taking the ring box and staring at it, as if studying it. "I can certainly say it's unique—couldn't be two like it, could there?"

"Hardly," Frost answered.

"Then you think perhaps this woman—your fiancee—somehow may have survived the bombing and this Fleisch woman might be able to shed some light on her whereabouts . . . Hmmm. Fascinating. Ahh—here we go." Frost looked around, the car stopping suddenly.

They were on the far side of the Glasgow airport as best as Frost could determine. "Helicopter here—taking us to Dunoon beyond the Firth of Clyde. Here's your ring, Captain Frost."

Frost followed Thurmond out of the car and limped across the field after him, the revolver—empty—back in one of his raincoat pockets.

Frost eyed the helicopter—aircraft wasn't his long suit, but he recognized the craft as a Boeing-Vertol CH-47C Chinook, the British military having purchased quite a few of the bus-like looking twin-rotor helicopters over the last decade. He had been aboard aircraft in the series several times in Viet Nam. "Where's the rest of the army we're taking with us?" Frost shouted to Thurmond, the inspector glancing back toward him and smiling enigmatically.

Thurmond disappeared inside the machine and Frost followed, looking behind him once and determining that for some reason his luggage wasn't following along. As Frost stepped inside the machine, he stopped. Thurmond was stripping away his hat and overcoat, pulling on a black, down jacket. "A few of us decided that if you walked in on that place by yourself, Captain—well, you'd be dead. I know that Mademoiselle Guttierez from several times our chaps have worked with the French on these terrorist matters. She sort of filled me in, so to speak. Meet my friends," and Thurmond gestured broadly around him.

There were two dozen men, clad in black coveralls and flak jackets and watch caps, Browning High Powers slung in shoulder holsters over the flak jackets and a collection of non-standard looking weapons festooning the men in a variety of positions—Bowie sized knives strapped to a thigh, a second handgun in a hip holster, one even wearing two shoulder rigs. Across his lap or between his knees, each man carried a Sterling L2A3 submachinegun. As Frost moved closer toward Thurmond, the man handed him a submachinegun. "That revolver is terribly nice, old boy—but this has a bit more firepower." It was a L34A1 submachinegun, the integral silencer version of the Sterling the others carried. "You go in with this, flak jacket and a few other niceties and we'll be three minutes behind you. Shouldn't get yourself in too much trouble in three minutes. And don't go thinking that a clandestine assault against an armed position expecting us is foolhardy—these chaps are all volunteers. Three minutes after you reach the house, we move out—should give you your ten minutes, but with a bit of an edge. Welcome aboard," and Thurmond extended his hand. Frost took it.

191

Chapter Twenty-Four

Frost flexed his left knee, walking on it in a tight circle near Thurmond and his Special Flying Squad. The borrowed black coveralls were a good enough fit and the watch cap, the black cloth gloves with the fingers cut away and the combat boots—a little tight but satisfactory—reminded him of other nights and other places, other times he'd gone in alone on an enemy. The leg would slow him up, but then he usually didn't have the benefit of a flak jacket, he convinced him-self—maybe the two would even out. The camouflage stick on his face and the backs of his fingers itched. Someday, he decided, he'd find somebody who made the stuff without whatever it was to which he was allergic. He'd checked the Sterling silenced subgun, was satisfied with it as well. A borrowed Parkerized FN High Power was in a borrowed military style shoulder holster under his left arm and the Metalife Custom .357 was hidden under the flak jacket inside his coveralls on his trouser belt—just in case. One of Thurmond's men had insisted on lending him a Fairbairn-Sykes type commando knife and Frost had taken it, though the knife style had never been something he'd particularly favored—the tang leading up into the handle section was too slim, he'd always felt. This strapped to his right thigh, he tried convincing himself—still walking—that he was ready for everything and anything. He shrugged. Most everything, he decided.

"Getting about time for you, Captain Frost," Thurmond announced coming up on him.

The one-eyed man turned, staring away from Thurmond and toward the blocked off and deserted street at the center of which was the house where Carlotta Fleisch and her bomb factory were located. "Godspeed to you," and Thurmond extended his hand.

Frost took it, saying, "I didn't expect this, expected to sort of walk in there alone and play it by ear. I owe you one, you and your men, however this turns out."

"I hope you find what you're looking for, Captain—few of us do, you know."

Frost only nodded. He gave his left leg one more flex—it hurt but he could move it. "I'm ready whenever you and your men are, Inspector."

"We'll move out then," and Thurmond, a flak vest over his down jacket strode along the wet sidewalk and out into the street, Frost, the Sterling in his right fist, a few paces behind. There had been a picture of Carlotta Fleisch, waiting for him

193

when Veronique had accompanied him to the military airfield just outside Istanbul. He recalled the picture now, stopping beside Thurmond alongside the police barricade. She had dark hair—brown probably, blue eyes, but nothing about her physically seemed to be at all remarkable as best he could remember.

Frost stared down the wet street, feeling the light touch of cold rain on his face. He could see the house, two story and frame, old looking. During the time aboard the military helicopter to Dunoon, Thurmond had shown Frost an artist's rendering of the interior of the two-story house, assembled after interviewing an elderly couple who had lived there for twenty years or more. On the main floor was a living room or parlor, fronting onto the street, and across from this, also fronting the street, a dining room. Behind the dining room was the huge kitchen, and opposite it in the central hallway and positioned behind the parlor was a single bedroom. But between the bedroom and the parlor was a single bathroom, the only one in the house. The second floor held four bedrooms, all off a second central hallway. There was a peaked roof and beneath it, between it and the second floor, was an unfinished attic.

Frost tried to visualize the layout in greater detail as he took the climbing rope Thurmond handed him, then hitched it over his left shoulder. Windows were off the unfinished attic, but they probably didn't open. Frost shouldered the light day pack, shifting the rope, then settling it again.

"Ready?"

"Ready," Frost almost whispered, feeling, hearing the tension in his voice.

"Ten minutes. I have five before the hour."

Frost glanced down to his wrist, rolling back the knit cuff of the black coverall, studying the Rolex. With his right hand, he depressed the elapsed time bezel circumferencing the case, moving the white luminous dot above the minute hand. "Ten minutes," Frost repeated. "From now."

Without another word, Frost started into a dead run along the police line and toward the opposite end of the street, then moved into the shadow of a gangway between two houses, his leg paining him. He ran down the gangway and to a tall unpainted board fence, jumping, grasping for the top of the fence and flipping over it into almost total darkness. He came down hard on his leg, wincing with the pain. He kept running toward the next fence line, this one lower, flipping it, landing awkwardly in a leafless hedgerow and pushing through it, across a postage stamp sized yard, tripping once on a bicycle left in the darkness, then across the muddy grass squishing under his feet toward the next fence. This one was high again, like the first fence, and Frost jumped, grasping for the top of the fence, hauling himself over it and dropping down into the darkness on the other side.

He rolled back the knit cuff on the coverall again. The plan was ten minutes, which really meant fourteen. Four minutes were allowed for Frost to reach the roof of the house where Carlotta Fleisch was hiding. The luminous face of the

Rolex showed two of those four minutes gone. In another minute, Thurmond and his Flying Squad would be starting, half along the front on the street side and half through the back yards, the route Frost had taken.

As he crouched in the darkness, the pain in his left leg came strong. He gritted his teeth against it, forcing himself to stand. The back porch was just as the drawing had shown it. The old fashioned kind with a high railing and a modest amount of gingerbread trim hanging down from the porch roof under the eaves.

Frost ran toward the porch, grasping the railing, testing it against his weight, then pulling himself up, flipping over it onto the porch. Heavy drapes seemed to cover the windows, one thin shaft of yellowish light filtering into the semi-darkness of the porch. Frost ignored it, getting his feet up onto the railing and standing, reaching up for the porch roof, finding a handhold and starting to pull himself up.

The Sterling clanged against the edge of the porch roof once and Frost froze, not daring to move. But there was no sound from the house, other than the muted, almost humming sound of a radio or television he had heard ever since entering the yard.

The one-eyed man started to move again, swinging his left leg up onto the porch roof, the pain forcing him to close his eye against it. He rolled onto his back, the coverall almost instantly saturating with water gathered there on the roof. Pushing himself to his hands and knees he edged across the roof. A tin roof by the feel and sound of it as he moved, it was slippery with the misty rain falling. He reached the rear side of the house, a lighted window with closed venetian blinds the only break in the house wall.

Frost gradually slipped the daypack from his shoulders, finding the grappling hook there and securing it to the end of the climbing rope.

Slowly, he edged along the roofline to the far side of the house. He glanced at his Rolex—one of his ten minutes was gone. "Dammit," he muttered. He looked up along the side of the house toward the shadowy darkness of the peaked roof. Shrugging, he let out a length of the climbing rope, then started to swing the hook, snapping the rope upward. The hook impacted against the side of the roof and skidded down along it—the noise it made seeming deafening to him in the otherwise almost total quiet.

"Had to have heard it," he muttered again. But it was an old house, there would be settling and creaking noises all the time. He hauled the hook back up, then started swinging it again, pendulum fashion below him. He heard the sound before he saw the light, a crunching of gravel beneath him.

The flashlight beam hit him square in the face. He heard a voice. *"Was ist los?"*

Frost swung the grappling hook back, hard, toward the sound of the voice. There was a clanging sound, as of metal striking metal, and then a groan. He peered over the roof and toward the ground, the flashlight lay there and in its glow he could see part of the outline of a body.

197

There was noise coming from inside the house now. "The hell with it," Frost whispered to himself. Climbing the roof, coming in through the attic window then down from the trap door into the second floor hall—that had been the plan.

He shrugged his shoulders, moved across the tin roof as fast as he could and swung the Sterling on line into an assault position under his right arm. He was opposite the venetian blind covered window and, his feet squared, he slipped the safety on the submachinegun and fired.

The glass seemed to disintegrate, the slats of the blinds dancing wildly under the impact of the metal jacketted 9mm solids. Frost rammed the wire stock of the subgun against the top of the window, knocking out a jagged shard of glass there, then pushed aside the blinds and jumped through.

The door into the hallway was open, the bed looking as though it had just been vacated, a table lamp lit, a book lying on one of the pillows, opened. Frost started across the room, glancing toward the book—he caught the name "Lenin". He decided he wouldn't have wanted to have read it—he knew the ending.

He reached the hall, standing there a moment in the bedroom doorway, orienting himself, then started down the hallway, limping as he ran. He could see the top of the stairs, heard a bolt clicking back on a subgun. Frost fired, before he even acquired the target. A red-haired woman, a scarf over her head, was standing just below the top stair, firing a submachinegun. Frost's first burst hit the top of the cutout for the stairwell, plaster smashing down from it. Frost fired again, the woman tumbling back out of sight. He could still hear the subgun firing over the banging sound of the body rolling down the stairs.

Frost wheeled, the bedroom door beside him opening. He started firing the Sterling, catching a man, wearing nothing but a pair of shorts, square in the chest, the body tumbling back. There was a woman behind the man, a pistol in her hand and Frost saw the face—Carlotta Fleisch. He hesitated, then felt something hammering down on him, on the back of his neck, darkness starting to wash over him as he tried to do something with the subgun—but he couldn't remember what . . .

Chapter Twenty-Five

Frost moved his head, opened his eye. His neck was stiff. He focused as he moved his left hand, trying to find his watch. The ten minutes was up. Gunfire—he remembered now. Hearing it had started to bring him around. He looked past his watch and across the room. It was the parlor, he decided. There were two people—a man and a woman, crouched by the base of the stairs, firing submachineguns up the stairwell. He could hear glass breaking. Frost shook his head to clear it. The windows in the parlor were shot out, there was little light in the house—one swaying bulb overhead in a shattered glass chandelier.

Subguns were rattling almost ceaselessly. There were men and women crouched by the windows, firing into the street. Frost started to move, then felt something cold against his temple. Slowly, he turned his head. Crouching over him as he lay on the floor was a woman, the same woman he'd seen in the upstairs doorway—Carlotta Fleisch.

"We kept you alive—perhaps as a hostage. But I think a hostage will do us no good. We will detonate some of the bombs in a matter of moments. Then all the explosives here will go. We can destroy perhaps a quarter of the city."

Frost turned his head to see her better, and as he did, he could see boxes of explosives behind her. There had to be more if what she was saying wasn't only wind. "Carlotta Fleisch?"

"Yes—I don't care who you are. But you are not a policeman. They don't take one-eyed men."

"Their misfortune," Frost answered, trying to smile. "Gonna kill me, right?"

"Of course."

"Tell me something first."

"You are crazy—the walls are filling with bullet holes, the second wave of the police assault will come in seconds. There are police on the upstairs floor. You will die now."

She cocked the hammer on the Walther P-38 in her right hand. "Wait—the ring you gave your boyfriend—Kolner—before he was killed. Where'd you get it?"

"Are you mad?"

"Where," and Frost sat up, despite the muzzle of the pistol at his head, his hands trembling as he wanted to reach for her, to throttle the information out of her.

"A woman reporter—a Jew I think. She followed me out of a department store in London. Recognized me, tried to stop me when the bomb blast went off. Called me a murderer, started screaming it at me. The whole block was on fire, there was rubble still falling from the secondary explosions. I shot .her in the head and she fell down on the body of a dead child. I saw the ring—I liked it and took it. Why?"

Frost let out a long sigh. Bess was dead. He heard the shouted word as if it was coming from someone else rather than himself. "Die!" His hand reached for the throat, the Walther going off and almost deafening him, a burning feeling in his chest as his fingers closed on Carlotta Fleisch's throat, squeezing it, his thumbs pressed against the Adam's apple, crushing the windpipe. The face was turning blue. The gun was firing again and Frost felt a pain in his abdomen. "Die!" he shouted again. The gunfire didn't matter—with all the submachinegun fire no one would hear it. The face was purple now, the tongue lolling out and thick, spit and blood starting to spill out of the corner of the mouth. He could see her pistol again out of the corner of his eye, but the hand loosened on it and the gun fell away. His fingers knotted around the terrorist woman's neck, lacing together as he squeezed, starting to smash the head against the carpeted floor, the eyes wide and bulging now, as if they were going to pop out of the head.

Frost let go, falling back on his haunches. The sound of the gunfire had slowed and he looked up, around him. There was a man bending over one of the boxes of explosives, just staring at him. Some of the others in the room were staring at him as well.

"Bess," Frost murmured, then threw himself across the floor toward a subgun lying there on the carpet. Maybe his movement broke the spell, he thought. But someone started shooting, Frost feeling the slugs ripping into his left side as his fingers closed around the submachinegun. He rolled and started shooting, a burst of automatic weapons fire hammering into him, knocking him back against the bullet pocked wall, but the subgun in his hands still firing.

The man beside the explosives boxes went down. Then a woman near the furthest window, her own submachinegun tearing into the floor at her feet and into the man beside her. Frost was still firing.

He tried to stand, seeing blood dripping from his left arm, seeing it smear on the floral patterned wallpaper on the wall beside him. There was another subgun and he picked it up as another burst tore into him and he doubled over. But he had the second submachinegun, then started firing it. The man, the woman—the two guarding the stairwell and shooting up toward the second floor where the police were. The man fell across the stairs, his throat pumping blood where Frost had shot him, the woman firing at Frost, then going down when Frost connected and she didn't.

Frost got to his knees, still firing, hearing shouts from the stairwell. Frost pumped the trigger of his subgun once more—nothing happened.

There was a woman shooting at him, but she fell down—he didn't know why. But it looked like a good idea to him and he fell down too and closed his eye . . .

Chapter Twenty-Six

There had been four operations to remove bullet fragments and repair intestinal damage. Frost remembered every one of them as he sat in his wheelchair on the veranda. It was a sunny day for a change and not too cool. The nurse had insisted on the blanket across his lap and despite the fact he had originally objected, he was glad for it now as the wind blew across the hospital grounds. Andrew Deacon of Diablo Protective Services had flown to London and visited him a week earlier. Whenever he wanted, his old job was waiting for him. Mike O'Hara, his friend from the FBI, had called the hospital, telling Frost to get well, telling Frost that when he finally was discharged from the hospital and came back stateside they could go get drunk together.

The commander of the Flying Squad—Inspector Thurmond—had visited twice, once officially to debrief Frost and once just to check in on his progress. The last thing Frost remembered before falling down in the old house in Dunoon was hearing shouting from the stairwell. Inspector Thurmond had filled him in on what had happened. The three men—three had been killed—who'd made it to the second floor had been trapped there, but when Frost had killed the man and woman guarding the stairwell, they'd charged down to the first floor and cleaned up the terrorist defenders. One of the terrorists had been trying to set off the explosives in the parlor, but hadn't made it. Aside from four dead and three wounded in the Flying Squad, the operation had been a total success. According to Thurmond, despite anything the doctors might have said, it was the flak jacket that had saved Frost. And even then it was a miracle. Frost had told Thurmond that a miracle like that wasn't what he'd wanted.

At that Thurmond had clapped him on the shoulder and left.

Frost lit a cigarette and stared across the veranda, toward the budding trees at the far end of the greenway.

His thoughts had drifted to Thurmond and the whole thing with the terrorists because this day was supposedly his last in the hospital. The nurse with the blonde hair and big brown eyes who liked bathing him so much had told him that, that she'd seen his chart and knew the way the doctor worked. Frost glanced at his watch now, the plastic hospital I.D. bracelet in the sun. He wanted to rip it off. It would be another hour before the doctor would make his afternoon visit and Frost suddenly realized how anxious he was to leave the place that had been his home for eight weeks.

He exhaled hard, stubbing out his cigarette in the plastic ashtray on the glass topped patio table. "Why do I want to leave?" he asked himself half-aloud. He had no desire to get back to work at Diablo, no desire to get drunk' with Mike O'Hara—he had no desire at all, he realized.

When Carlotta Fleisch had told him she'd shot Bess in the head, it had drained from him all the desire.

After the bombing, the thought of revenge had kept him going. After the recovery of the ring he'd given Bess and the slight chance she was somehow still alive, the hope of finding her had kept him going. But he had strangled her murderer, and confirmed Bess's death.

All he had left was the ring, locked in the hospital safe now.

"Depression," he murmured. He had been down before—in the days when he'd used the bottle to keep himself going, the days before he'd turned mercenary, then became involved with Diablo Protective Services. He'd been down when he'd lost his eye, realizing that for the rest of his life he'd be half blind. He'd taught himself rudimentary braille once, out of fear that someday the other eye would be lost.

There was still pain in his abdomen from the surgery, still soreness in his left leg—which had been shot up again when he'd gone down in the terrorist bomb factory.

But there was nothing.

Frost stared across the grass at the trees again. There was still the house an old friend had offered to lend him, the place in New Mexico above Albuquerque. He could go there. But then do what, he wondered?

He could try to find the French girl, Veronique. She had written him once in the hospital. He shrugged off the idea. Perhaps someday, but not now—

"Frost—I say, you're looking fit today."

Frost turned around, awkwardly in the wheelchair. It was Thurmond. "Inspector—gonna try to cheer me up again?"

"Don't think I'll have to, actually. You were supposed to be discharged from the hospital tomorrow—called your doctor. Hope you don't mind?"

"No; nobody tells me anything around here anyway."

"But you're getting out today—this afternoon, actually. There's something you've got to do."

"I thought all the paperwork on that deal with the terrorists was done?"

Thurmond nodded his head thoughtfully. "It is—but there's something else. Not that I can't tell you, but I won't. Not the sort of thing to talk about, actually."

"What the hell are you saying?"

"Got someone for you to identify—tied in with this terrorist thing."

"I don't understand you."

"Simple—actually. Really just attempting to verify some information, you might say." Thurmond lit his pipe. Frost had always admired people who could keep a pipe going, especially without constantly sucking at it and making noises with it. "So, I'll call up the nurse, have you wheeled along. Get you—"

Frost pushed himself to his feet, the wheelchair slipping away from him as he did, his left leg hurting. "I don't need to be wheeled along!"

"There you go—wondered if you were still alive, old man."

Frost took a step closer to Thurmond. "What the hell is going on?"

"Some of the information regarding the terrorist activities—things pulled out of that house. Need your help in sorting through it. That's all. Thought you might be interested in getting out of here, doing something rather than sitting around and just vegetating. Up to you though. Planning to die right here in this chair, or do you plan to get out of it and move around and live and be worthwhile again? What that woman told you about your lady friend shattered you. You talked about it under the ether—"

"How the hell do you know—and they don't use ether anymore anyway."

"Whatever, old boy. But you did. Doctor discussed it with me since I was the one who was in charge of the operation at the house. Thought it might be official business. Told him it was so he'd tell me anything else you said. And he did."

"Thanks a lot," Frost snapped, turning away, trying to light a cigarette, walking toward the railing of the veranda. He was cold, shivering, but he didn't feel like showing it.

"A lot of men, good men, get themselves into something that's beyond them, get a personal problem that ruins them for the rest of their lives. You see it in police work, see it in war; some men come out of the rubble of their own lives and start over, some just sit around. What kind are you, Frost?"

Frost turned and looked at Thurmond, glaring at him. "Nobody's business but my own."

"What about that eye? Got out of that thing with your head on straight, didn't you? Could have taken out a good deal of lesser men. But not you. You've been shot up so many times the doctor said you have scars on top of scars. That means you've got a little sand—unless you lost it all back there in that house. Now what's it going to be—get out and do something useful to yourself, or just sit around and wait for people to feel sorry for you?"

"Okay; you show me what it is you want identified, or sorted out, or whatever—then butt out," Frost snapped. He started across the veranda, toward the glass doors leading back into the hospital wing. "I'll meet ya in the lobby," he shouted. What made him most angry was that he realized Thurmond was right.

Chapter Twenty-Seven

The drive cross-country in darkness was worse than the drive had been in twilight. Frost leaned back in the seat beside Thurmond and closed his eye, then opened it again. "How the hell long is this going to be?"

"A chap I once knew told me that profanity was the ignorant man's substitute for an adjective—you agree?"

"Shut up," Frost snapped, staring back at the window. "What is going on?"

"Here—you'll need this. Took it off your body before they carted you off to the hospital."

Frost could see it gleaming slightly in the greenish glow from the dashboard lights. Thurmond was fumbling in the briefcase between them, trying to drive at the same time. "And take these too." The first object was the custom .357 with his name on it, the gun his old friend Mahovsky had made for him. The other items were the speedloaders and the holster. "I loaded those speedloaders for you. There's more ammunition in the glove box in front of you."

"What's going on?" Frost asked, checking the gun by feel in the darkness. It was empty and he prodded one of the speedloaders against the cylinder star and charged the six holes, closing the cylinder tight and jamming the revolver into the holster. He kept it on his lap.

"Hadn't wanted to tell you—you've been so blasted persistent, though."

"Remember what you said about profanity."

"Quite; but I'll tell you if you promise not to go berserk."

"Tell me what?" Frost asked.

"That Fleisch woman—Carlotta Fleisch. She was lying to you. She was never in London at the time of the bombing. Couldn't have killed your lady friend then, could she?"

Frost shook—he felt like laughing, crying, throwing up—getting out of the moving car and screaming. "You've heard the one about the dying always telling the truth—makes me doubt death-bed statements."

"What?" Frost shook his head, thinking he wasn't hearing right.

"Had a lovely talk with that FBI chap you know—O'Hara. Even though he is Irish, I don't hold it against him. He's an American now."

"What's O'Hara got to—"

"Seems he called you, then decided to call me to see how you were really doing. One of those chaps who doesn't trust doctors, worried about your health. We got on rather well. Bizarre fellow, though. Got me thinking, talking about your dead lady friend and all, so I decided to make a preliminary check of the hospitals, just to see perhaps if anyone had a record of a gunshot wound that day matching up with what Carlotta Fleisch told you. No one did. Struck me as odd, so I backchecked Carlotta Fleisch. Your other lady friend—the French Mademoiselle—Veronique? She helped me there, tracing Carlotta Fleisch's movements; I suppose that's why I gave the stiff upper lip lecture. You thought this was all over. But it isn't.''

"What are you saying?" Frost asked, lighting a cigarette, his hands trembling so badly he almost dropped the lighter.

"Found they have a safe house they use here. Seems one of our rather important politicians is sympathetic to them, thinks they're some sort of people's army fighting for freedom and all that rubbish. He's a bit too important for me to get a search warrant and officially I can't just break down his door without enough evidence. I don't have it. Your terrorist bomber was a chap named van Brach. If anyone killed your lady friend Bess, he did. He's up at the house along with about a half dozen or more of his terrorist friends. Since I couldn't go in officially, I did the next best thing. Kept them under surveillance, then contacted your friend O'Hara—wanted to see if he had any vacation time coming. By curious coincidence he did. He's been keeping tabs as you Yanks say—keeping tabs on the house for the last three days. Today was the first I could get you out of the hospital.

You and I—and your friend O'Hara are going to do something quite illegal—"

"Look—no sense putting your neck on the line," Frost said. "I can get this von Brach character myself. If what you're doing is illegal, let me take—"

"Just what I thought you'd say—got your handle back on life, what?"

Frost looked at the man, saying nothing.

"I got the chap who runs the hospital finance office to open the safe. You might need this too." He shoved something into Frost's hands. Frost could tell it by the feel. It was the velvet box with the ring. "That's the reason why your Mr. O'Hara and I are coming along to help. There've been persistent reports of a blonde haired woman sighted near the house, always with one or two of von Brach's people. And we've made a background check on all of von Brach's associates. Shouldn't be a blonde there. Got a rather fuzzy photo of the woman—could be your lady. Alive."

"Stop the car a second."

"What?"

"Stop the car!" Frost insisted. Thurmond pulled over. Frost wrenched the door handle, throwing the door open and stepping out, fumbling the gun and the ring and everything else Thurmond had given him into his pockets, then walking back along to the rear fender, leaning on it, breathing hard. "Jesus . . ." Frost shook his head, trying to make himself breathe the right way.

He could hear Thurmond behind him. "Are

you all right, old boy?"

Frost couldn't talk—he just nodded his head and tried breathing.

Chapter Twenty-Eight

Frost stood on the hillside, looking across the road and toward the ocean and the solitary, almost classic English country home there, a few lights on along the second floor, one light on the first floor. Frost inhaled hard, his palms sweating on the silenced Sterling L34A1 subgun.

"I hate automatics—lend me your revolver, sport—huh?"

Frost looked to his right, smiling. "O'Hara— I'd lend you almost anything. But not the revolver. It's—kind of a personal thing, I think. Funny maybe; but a friend made it for me, and I think he'd want me using it tonight. You know?"

"Yeah—yeah. Excuses, excuses." O'Hara turned away, muttering.

Frost turned away from the house, looking at Thurmond. "I feel good—better than I have for a long time. I think she's there. I almost feel it."

Thurmond only nodded. Frost smiled to himself; he wondered if you could get high on adrenalin. He felt that way.

"From what your man O'Hara tells me, I understand you're more experienced at this commando sort of thing than I am. What do we do first, Captain?"

Frost smiled broadly. "Well—you brought the guns, the ammo, the flak jackets, even the ski masks so if any of them are alive when we get out, they won't be able to get that creep politician to pin anything on the cops. I think you did okay. I studied the layout you had in the car. I think I figured it out. Just relax—it'll all be perfect."

"You sound a good bit different, my friend," Thurmond noted.

"I feel a good bit different. Whether she's alive or dead, I'm gonna make it. And she's alive. I'm going in there, gonna find her and give her back her ring."

"Jees—you're goin' mushy in the head, Frost," O'Hara groused.

Frost just patted O'Hara on the back. "Maybe so. But I feel good. We're going down there in a couple of minutes, going over the wall, get inside and get her out."

"Just like that, huh—man?"

Frost grinned at O'Hara, then softly, not looking at O'Hara, but at the house instead he said, "Just like that—just like that . . ."

Chapter Twenty-Nine

Frost hugged the cast iron grillwork fence, catching his breath. The weeks in the hospital had slowed him up. He shrugged, smiling under the ski mask that covered his face. He started running again, along the fenceline, toward the trees. He stopped again, catching his breath, glancing from side to side in the darkness, seeing no one, hearing no one. There should be two guard dogs, two sentries at the most.

Frost took a meter length of rope, knotted into a loop and flipped it up onto the spike at the top of the fence four feet above his head, reaching out to maximum extension with his arms and hauling himself up. Unless an electronic security system had been installed on the fence since earlier that morning when O'Hara had checked it, there would be none now.

Frost reached the top of the fence, clambered over the spikes and jumped from a crouch to the ground ten feet or so below him. The noise of his feet hitting the ground had sounded loud to him, but he reasoned probably no one else had heard it.

He swung the Sterling off his back, working the safety, starting forward hugging a stand of scrub trees, moving in a low crouch.

The one-eyed man ducked into the brush a moment, hearing the crunching of gravel. He ticked off the possibilities. O'Hara and Thurmond were coming in on the far side of the house, on the sea side, so to have heard them would have been impossible. One of the sentries, probably with a dog. Frost edged deeper into the brush, finding the hilt of the borrowed knife Thurmond had given him, a Bowie pattern, large, the false edge sharpened.

He heard the snorting sound before he heard the footfalls, wheeled and thrust the knife forward, edge up. The black Doberman was coming down on him, fangs bared, the only sound, the sound of its breathing as Frost let it fall on the knife.

There was a solitary yelp and Frost pulled the knife and edged into the bushes. "Max—return! Max—return!"

There was a slight Germanic lilt to the voice—more Austrian sounding to Frost than actual German. "Max?"

"He couldn't make it," Frost smiled, stepping out of the shadows, the silenced Sterling bucking in his hands, a perfect three-shot burst cutting a swatch across the chest and neck of the dog handler, the man starting for his submachinegun but never quite making it.

The man was still alive as he tumbled in a heap to the ground. Frost snapped the skeletonized stock of the subgun against the side of the man's head—he fixed the still alive part.

Frost moved ahead, toward the house, banking that the other sentry and the second guard dog would be on the far side of the house, on the seaward side where Thurmond and O'Hara could deal with them.

Frost ran along the hedgerows of the immaculate, formal garden, each sculptured hedge a monument to someone's having labored tirelessly over it. One of the terrorists apparently did the work since keeping a staff and armed men with guard dogs would have been impossible. Frost smiled as he ran, thinking about the hedgerows. He'd plant whoever had clipped them under them if he could.

There was a stone railing and beyond it a flagstone surfaced terrace. Frost shrugged as he ran toward it. He felt good tonight. He ran to the railing and vaulted over it, coming down in a low crouch beyond it. His left leg hurt, but he ignored it. His abdomen ached near the scar from the last operation, but the stitches were out. He couldn't worry about it.

Glass french doors were at the far end of the terrace, light filtering from behind them. All other light was still on the second floor of the house. He stopped beside the doors. He felt along them, his fingers and his eye inspecting them for an alarm system. They were confident, the terrorists. They had to be, he thought. He smiled again. He took the Bowie knife and passed the blade over the doors where they joined. "Hmm," he murmured.

He'd seen it in a movie once. He took the knife, forced the blade between the two doors and hammered it down, hearing the lock breaking. He felt himself smile again, then pulled the doors outward toward him. The Sterling in an assault position, he stepped through into the light, then going into a roll across the carpeted floor. There was no one.

Frost got to his feet and walked across the room, his hands in the fingerless gloves pulling the doors shut. He started back across the room. It was a library. "What if—" he heard himself mutter. What if it were not Bess? What if it were a Bess who'd been tortured, brutalized? Why had they kidnapped her if it were her?

He shrugged it off, realizing that he had to believe.

He reached the library doors, listening. He glanced at the Rolex on his left wrist under the black knit shirt he wore. O'Hara and Thurmond should be coming up on the other side of the house. Then in two minutes more they'd come in. Before then, he had to reach Bess, to keep the terrorists from killing her.

He inhaled hard, filling his chest, taking a step back away from the double library doors, then moving toward them, turning the door handle, opening the one to his right a crack, then peering past it into the hallway. The floor was like a checkerboard of brown and gold tiles, an elaborate mantel dominating the far wall of what seemed to be a windowless hallway. There was brilliant light streaming down from an elaborate, likely genuine crystal chandelier. Frost opened the door wider, looking from side to side. There was no one.

Frost stepped into the hallway, then froze. He could hear footsteps in the hallway, coming from the rear of the house. He swung the Sterling back and flattened himself against the library doors. The footsteps were getting louder. He saw the figure, saw the face as it turned toward him; his hands reached out, his left fist knotting on the windpipe of the blond-haired man, his right fist hammering forward, smashing the base of the nose, breaking the bone and driving it up between the sinuses and into the brain. The eyes—blue—were suddenly wide open in death.

Frost caught the body before it fell, dragged it toward the library doors and dropped it in a heap inside on the carpeted floor.

The one-eyed man closed the library doors, then started for the stairway, swinging the Sterling back into an assault position, taking the treads of the circular staircase two at a time, hugging the wall side to avoid any creaking sound.

He glanced down at his watch, the ski mask making his face itch and sweat. O'Hara and Thurmond had one more minute. Frost continued up the stairs, stopping at eye level to the second floor, peering ahead.

He saw no one. He started to move, then wheeled, falling back across the steps.

"Hey—you!"

There was a man at the base of the stairs, a pistol in his right hand. Frost buzzed the Sterling at him, the sound of the silenced 9mm subgun like

221

a long, loud belch. The man crumpled to the floor, Frost pushed himself up and ran. No one would have heard the shots, but the shout the man had made before Frost had shot him—that would have been heard.

Frost had gambled, from the layout of the house deciding one of the two rooms between the lighted rooms would have been where they kept Bess. He passed the first doorway and the second—the second, one of the lighted rooms. He could hear noise from inside it.

He stopped in front of the next door, took a half step back and kicked his left foot against the doorlock.

"Ouch!" he muttered. It didn't always work. Cursing, he pumped a burst from the subgun into the lock, the door springing inward, Frost throwing himself through into the darkness. He snatched at the Kel-Lite flashlight in his belt and swept it across the room. It was empty—a storeroom. "Dammit!"

The one-eyed man raced back into the hallway, the door next to him opening now, a man and a woman coming from it, the man with a pistol in his hand. Frost fired the Sterling. The woman screamed, the man died.

Frost wheeled, racing to the next door, wondering if it were too late to pray he'd guessed right on the two unlighted rooms. He started to kick at the door, then raised the submachinegun. There was sound to his left, gunfire. He dove to the floor, the wall where his head had been ripping apart, two men with submachineguns at the head of the

222

stairs. Frost fired his Sterling, nailing the first man, the subgunner falling back down the stairs.

The second man pulled back out of Frost's line of fire.

There was a series of short, staccato pistol shots. "FBI—kiss off, sucker!"

"O'Hara," Frost laughed.

"Damnfool automatics," Frost heard the distant voice shout.

Frost got to his feet. Whoever had counted the terrorists at the house had erred, he realized. There was more gunfire from the base of the stairs, the belching sounds of Thurmond's Sterling, identical to the one Frost carried, and the sounds of O'Hara's borrowed FN High Power.

Frost started to shoot the doorlock; then stepped back. He kicked out with his right foot this time, the lock holding but the doorframe around it splintering, the door swinging inward.

There was no light and Frost started in, the Kel-Lite in his left hand, the subgun with a fresh stick in it in his right. He tripped over something on the floor, heard a groaning sound and flashed the light on it.

He could feel cold sweat on his face. He ripped the ski mask away. If he'd shot through the door . . . "Bess—God Almighty—Bess!"

Her hair was dirty and longer than he'd remembered it. There was a bruise on her forehead. But her eyes, squinting against the flashlight beam, were bright, clear. "Bess . . ."

"If I say it's about time you showed up are you gonna slug me?"

"Shut up," he whispered, hauling her up from the mattress on the floor, holding her in his arms.

"Frost—thank you,—God, thank you, Frost," she whispered. He dropped his gun, taking her face in his hands, kissing her, feeling the wetness there on her face, tasting the salty taste of her tears.

"I gotta get you out of here—come on."

Frost started to his feet, snatching up his gun.

"Frost? If I could walk or stand up, don't you think I'd be doing it?"

Frost shone the light on her again and she squinted against it. Her ankles were bound together with a twist of rope, and her hands—in front of her—were cuffed together.

"Can't do anything about the cuffs, kid," he rasped. "But I can fix the feet."

Frost pulled the Bowie knife and hacked the rope, then hauled her up beside him. She fell against him. "They didn't walk me much today—I'm—"

"Come on," Frost rasped, pulling her toward him, bending, putting her up on his shoulder.

"Frost!"

"Relax—I just had eight weeks rest."

Bess over his left shoulder, the Sterling in his right hand, Frost started into the hallway.

He started toward the stairs.

"Frost!"

Frost started to wheel when he heard her scream, remembered too late she was on his shoulder and tripped with her, swinging the Sterling but getting the sling caught up in the chain on the handcuffs.

·"You must be her rescuer. How nice you can die together."

The man at the back of the hall was tall, dark haired, black eyed and his description matched the verbal picture Thurmond had given of van Brach, the terrorist bomber.

Frost punched the Metalifed Custom Special out to arm's length in his left hand and blew off the top of van Brach's head.

Chapter Thirty

"No—of course I don't have a handcuff key. I'm no damned police equipment store."

"I'm afraid I didn't bring one either—perhaps back at the car, though."

"A couple of fine cops you guys are," Frost laughed, holding Bess in his arms

"You want to know what happened?"

"In a second, kid," Frost told her. "Got something you lost," and Frost found the worn velvet box in his pocket, took the gold ring with the roaring tiger's mouth with the diamond set in it, then placed it on the third finger of her left hand.

She leaned up to him, her handcuffed wrists scooping over his head, her hands on his neck, then kissed him hard.

"You know—you guys got a lot of time for this—later, right?" O'Hara sounded disgusted, Frost thought.

"You're right—we better get out of here,"

Frost said, unhooking Bess's wrists from his neck.

They started across the grass. "What did happen?"

"You want the short version or the dynamite exclusive I'm gonna do called, 'I Was A Prisoner of The People's Army'? I can give you either one," she laughed.

She was still weak, Frost decided, feeling her stumble against him. "Are your feet cold—barefoot I mean?"

"It feels so good to walk—I don't care that I'm barefoot."

"Well; what happened," O'Hara snapped with his usual impatience.

"I'll give you guys the short one," she said. "I left Frost and started for the bathroom when I saw van Brach coming out of the men's room right next to the ladies room. I'd interviewed van Brach once in prison a few years ago. I started after him. I was thinking about getting you," and she looked up at Frost. He liked her green eyes, drank them in. "But I figured there wasn't time. Figured I'd stop a cop. I was on the street when the bomb went off. I should have realized that was what he was doing there. But I didn't. Something must've hit me. When I woke up, I was strapped down on a stretcher in the back of an ambulance. I thought I was on my way to a hospital. My head hurt. But I guess I passed out again. Anyway, I woke up here. Van Brach had decided to keep me alive in case things got too hot and he needed leverage with the police to get out of the country. They were all working with the IRA people, everything."

"How did your ring get taken?" It was Thurmond.

"This woman Carlotta something—"

"Fleisch," Frost suggested.

"Yes—I think so. She saw the ring on my hand, almost cut off my finger getting it. Said she had someone who'd like it and I wasn't going to be needing it."

"Did they harm you?" Thurmond asked. "I don't intend to bring up an embarrassing subject or anything that will cause you—"

"No," she said, sounding puzzled to Frost. "That was the funny thing." She rubbed her head. "I got this thing two days ago. I tried to make a break for it and one of them hit me with the butt of a machinegun."

"Submachinegun," Frost corrected.

"It goes bang a lot when you pull the trigger once. I don't know. But no—they never," and she stopped and leaned against Frost. "Never did," she whispered.

"Good," he told her.

"Hey guys—not to break up the party," O'Hara began, stopping beside the Jaguar Frost and Thurmond had arrived in. "What do we do about all the dead people—those wonderful guys and gals who brought us terrorist bombings and kneecappings and lots of other good stuff?"

"I think we leave them right where they are, actually," Thurmond smiled, sitting down behind the steering wheel, the dome light lighting his face. "That chap I mentioned, who sympathizes with the IRA, the PFLFE, all those other left wing ter-

228

rorists groups? I think it would be perfectly lovely for him to motor up here next weekend as he usually does, find a houseful of corpses and bullet holes and try explaining it to the Yard. Actually, I'm rather anxious to hear what he says. Should be most entertaining. Wait a minute," and Thurmond leaned across to the glove compartment, searching it, then sat upright, holding out a small metallic object in his right hand. "I believe someone wanted a handcuff key?"

Chapter Thirty-One

There had been a session at a doctor's office in London, a doctor who was Thurmond's brother-in-law. He'd prescribed a vitamin supplement for Bess, but otherwise pronounced her sound after giving her a B-complex injection. Thurmond had had Frost's things checked into a hotel far from the center of London and it had been easy enough to get Bess—clothes ripped, wearing Frost's jacket, her face dirty, her hair ragged—in through a back door. For a supposedly staid British policeman, Frost had decided, Thurmond was quite surprising. Quite versatile as well.

Frost poured a glass full of scotch and a second one for Bess. "I haven't had anything with alcohol in it for—God! how long did they have me?"

"Too long," Frost told her, passing her the glass.

"I missed you," she told him. "I thought

maybe you'd given up on me."

"To tell the truth, I thought you were dead, lied to myself and told myself maybe you weren't, but then finally realized you had to be. Until today, with Thurmond."

"I was talking with O'Hara—he told me what you've been doing."

"When were you—"

"When you and Inspector Thurmond went into the doctor's office ahead of us. You took losing me hard. I guess I should be flattered."

"I don't wanna lose you again, kid."

"You won't," she smiled, sipping at the scotch. "Give me a cigarette?"

Frost nodded, taking two Camels out of the crumpled pack in his shirt pocket, then finding his lighter and firing them both. He handed one to Bess.

"O'Hara's funny," she mused. "I think he was so happy for us both all he could do was complain."

"Yeah," Frost nodded, thinking for a moment about the steely-eyed FBI man and the first moment O'Hara'd seen Bess was alive. Instinctively, O'Hara had put his arms around her, held her a moment, then started his usual complaining.

"I like your friend Inspector Thurmond—I guess he's the one who found me—I didn't know what to say to him to thank him."

"You don't need to thank him," Frost told her quietly.

"What about you? Do I thank you? How do I do it?"

Frost set his glass down and moved out of the chair, dropping to his knees beside her chair, taking her face in his hands and kissing her . . .

They'd showered together, re-exploring each other's bodies, talking, holding one another under the steaming water. Something about the night, Frost felt, had made them both realize there was no need to hurry.

By the time they left the bathroom, the sky outside the twelfth floor window was grayish blue with morning, the light filtering across the floor and the bed, across Bess's face as Frost stood holding her in his arms. They sat on the edge of the bed, Frost's hands moving across her breasts, her back, her abdomen. He leaned her back across the bed, his mouth on hers, feeling her hands on him, the tips of her fingers moving across the hairs of his chest. "You're getting grayer," she murmured.

Frost pushed up from her a moment, making a show of looking down at her, then whispering, "You're not."

"Hmm," she smiled, closing her eyes. Frost kissed her eyes, then her mouth as he slipped between her thighs . . .

The sun was stronger, but the sky still looked gray as Frost lay silently on the bed, Bess asleep finally in the crook of his right arm. On the bedside table was his lighter, a half-emptied pack of cigarette, his watch, the .357 Metalifed Custom and his eyepatch.

Something made the one-eyed man think that

life was somehow never going to be simple, or easy either. He had never wanted a life like that at any event. Doing what he did was as much a part of him now as was the eyepatch—he wondered if there were a commonality of reasons there too.

Some of his mail had tracked him down while he'd been in the hospital. There had been an invitation to a reunion of an old mercenary outfit he'd fought with in Africa, in the days when he'd just been getting started plying his trade. He hadn't really thought there were enough of the unit left alive to have a reunion in anything larger than a phone booth. But he thought about it now, perhaps taking Bess, to give them some time together without her office and without his life interfering either.

It would be good to get back to Africa. He'd met Bess there when he'd saved her life once before. A smile crossed his lips. It had been terrorists then as well.* She rolled over in his arm and he watched her left hand as it rested on the white sheet across her abdomen. His ring was back where it belonged.

*See, They Call Me The Mercenary #1, *The Killer Genesis*

233